DEFYING DESTINY

Forsaken Sinners MC Series: Book Three

By Shelly Morgan

DEFYING DESTINY

Limitless Publishing, LLC
Kailua, HI 96734
www.limitlesspublishing.com

Formatting: Limitless Publishing

ISBN-13: 978-1-68058-595-7
ISBN-10: 1-68058-595-9

DEDICATION

I want to dedicate this book to all those out there that have lost someone; whether it be from natural causes or something else. I hope you know that you are not alone.

CHAPTER 1

Louie

Age 17

One more hour, then I can finally go home and be away from this shithole. Then it's just one more month until graduation.

I fucking hate school—and I don't mean that in the way that most kids would probably say they hate school. I hate it because of the pieces of shit that roam these halls. They all walk around like they know everything and are the kings and queens of the town. But they ain't royalty. They are the shit on the bottom of my fucking boot. The pesky mosquitos that want to suck you dry.

My dad and I may be trailer park trash in their eyes, but we are better than *everyone* in this Godforsaken town. Better than the mayor who fucks his assistant on the side. Better than the preacher man who has a thing for little boys. And better than the teachers, the townsfolk, and their spawns.

1

I grew up without a mother and even though I wish I would have known her, I can't say that my life would have been any better or I would have felt more love in my life. My father provided everything for me. He was the one who taught me how to walk, talk, and ride a bike. He played catch with me when he wasn't working, helped with my homework when I needed it, and always made sure I had a hot meal at least once a day. My dad means everything to me and I'll wipe the floor with anyone who disrespects him. He was a God damn fucking Marine—served five tours overseas, took more than a dozen bullets throughout his service to this country, and saved more men than anyone will ever know. My dad is a fucking hero—*my* hero.

The bell ringing brings me out of my thoughts. One more class to go.

Getting out of my seat, I put all my books into my bag and make my way into the hall and toward my locker. Since my last period is Shop, I make sure to grab everything I need so I can leave right after class. Any extra time spent here is time wasted in my eyes, even if it's just to walk back to my locker. No fucking thank you.

I'm the first one into the shop, as usual, since I have no need to delay. I get right to work on the old Chevy Mr. Peterson brought in for us to work on. Today, we're starting to work on the engine.

Shop is actually one of my top favorite classes, the other being gym. Those are the classes I get to use my hands. In here, it's tearing shit apart, finding the problem, then fixing it. In gym, it's pushing my body to the limit and working my ass off. Usually, no matter what the activity is for that day, the gym teacher will let me do my own thing in the weight room. I think he's learned that I don't play well with others. Either that, or he just doesn't want to have to deal with me, like everyone else in this fucking place.

Five minutes later, the rest of the students show up. Not like they will actually do anything. But as long as they stay the fuck away from me, I'm good.

I've been finding it harder and harder to hold my tongue and I can only be pushed so far before I'll pull my hands out of my pockets and knock one of those fuckers out. Sometimes the beast inside me takes over and the rage is just too much. It's been there for as long as I can remember, waiting for the opportunity to bare its teeth and draw blood. But, for my dad's sake, I do my best to just let things slide. My dad taught me to turn the other cheek, but told me to stand my ground. Called it bein' a man. Said that if someone was wrong, to never back down and prove my point by driving it home. And if that meant throwing the first punch and whooping their ass, then so be it.

I told my dad that once I graduated, I wanted to move to the east or west coast. We've lived in Iowa my whole life, but I've always dreamed of being close to the ocean and away from this shit town. I want to find a good trainer wherever we find a decent place and start fighting for money. I've done a good job training myself in my homemade gym in my room and watching any video I can find, but if I want to make it professionally and make the big bucks, I'll have to find someone willing to train me.

I know I can do it too. I'm good enough even without professional training, but I'll need that to take me to the next level. Plus, in order to get signed up for the big money fights, it's easier to do if you have a trainer in your corner. Especially if that training has a big name.

Dad wasn't too open to the idea of moving away at first, but now that he knows I'm serious I think he's warming up to the idea. It's not like he'll have anything holding him here after I graduate and leave. I don't want to go without him, but I've told him that I will if I have to. I can't be here anymore. If I stay for even a day longer than necessary, I know I'll end up just like everyone says I will—dead or in jail—and I will *not* let that happen.

Feeling my phone vibrate in my pocket, I wipe off my hands and pull it out. It's a text message from my dad. He rarely ever messages me and for him to do so during school hours must mean it's important. I turn around to make sure Mr. Peterson isn't watching, then pull up the message.

Dad: Things are finally turning around for us, son. This should help for the big move, don't you think?

Attached to the message is a picture of him holding a lottery ticket and a huge fucking check for fifty thousand dollars.

Me: Is that for real?

Even though my dad has never played a trick on

me, at least not to this extent, I have to ask. I don't want to get excited, but looking at the picture, I know it's real before I even read his next text.

Dad: It's real and it's ours. So here's to the future.

I don't even bother responding. Instead, I grab my bag and am out the door before my teacher even realizes I'm leaving.

Sprinting out to my banged-up truck, I throw my book bag inside before jumping in after it. I burn rubber as I press down on the accelerator and speed home. I only live about five minutes from school, but today I make it there in two.

As soon as I pull in front of the house beside my dad's old Harley, the door opens and I see him standing there with the biggest smile I think I've ever seen on him. "You just couldn't wait an hour, could ya." It's not a question, but a statement.

Getting out of the truck I walk up to him and pull him in for a tight hug. Most kids my age, guys especially, don't hug their parents anymore, but not me. I love my dad more than anything and have never been shy about showing it to him or anyone else.

"What the fuck do you think, old man?" I answer him anyway.

My dad laughs and shakes his head. One of the best things about him is he never scolds me for swearing. He always said that if you're man enough to swear in front of your elders without fear of being punished, then you're man enough to actually say it. Yeah, my dad's pretty fucking awesome, I know.

"So we going out to celebrate?" I ask. Things have always been tight in our house—he works almost sixty hours a week to make sure we can make rent and that I have food in my stomach and clothes on my back. It would be nice to go out and have a nice meal for a change, instead of eating ramen noodles or Hamburger Helper.

"You read my mind, boy," he says before heading back into the house.

"I was thinking we'd go to that steakhouse downtown and then I was thinking of stopping by the bar for a celebratory drink." He's hesitant when he says this, but it's only because I know he feels like he shouldn't waste money on something as trivial as alcohol when he could put it to better use. Usually that better use is something for me or paying bills.

I look at him with a stern look. "Don't you even think about taking that back. Hell yeah you should go get a drink. Shit, maybe you can get me a six-pack before you go and I can have a celebratory drink too." I end on a laugh, which has him laughing too.

"Yeah. I can do that, son. But no driving, ya hear?" Now it's his turn to use a stern look. The one major rule my father has is no drinking and driving. He'd say, "If you want to have a drink here and there, that's fine, but I need to know where you are and I better not ever catch you behind the wheel after you've even had a sip. You call me, I don't care what time it is, I'll come and get your ass.

Better me than the police or the morgue." I don't go out drinking a lot because let's face it, I couldn't care less about going to any of the parties the kids my age attend, but I have on occasion gone out to the bluffs with a few cans of beer to just clear my head and think about the future. And I've never once gone against his word—I either walk home or I call him. He's never gotten mad when I've asked him to come get me, even if it was past two in the morning and he had to be up at five.

"I hear ya, old man. Now let's go. I'm fucking hungry and I can hear a big-ass steak callin' my name." Even though it's barely four, we're used to eating early whenever we're both home at night. Dad usually goes to bed around six-thirty since he has to be up at the ass crack of dawn. He doesn't have to work tomorrow since it will be Saturday and it's his weekend off, but I figure we might as well keep with our usual eating schedule. I'm also hoping there won't be a lot of people there since it's earlier than most people eat. I don't want anyone to ruin our good mood and a good meal.

Since I know he wants to stop at the bar later, we both hop into my truck. He's an adult but he's never driven after he's had a drink. I think that's one of his best qualities; he won't do something that he tells me or others not to. He says if it's important enough for him to tell others, then he needs to take his own words to heart too. Most people will tell others what to do just because they enjoy feeling like they are the boss, but then they don't do the same. Fucking hypocrites.

On the drive over, we talk about mindless shit,

7

like how his work week went or how school and training is going for me. I've never had a problem talking to my dad about anything. I guess you could say we're closer than most father/son relationships usually are. I will always think of him as my father, but he's my best friend too. I know that he would never judge me and he'll always give me advice or direction when asked or if he feels it's needed.

Once we park and head inside, we're immediately seated.

"Out celebrating, eh, Mike?" I hear someone say from behind me as we sit down.

I look over my shoulder and see that it's Marcus Brindel. He's the town attorney and father to Jimmy, who is my age and the star quarterback for the high school football team.

My dad laughs, though it's a little strained. He hates these people almost as much as I do, maybe sometimes even more. "Well, can ya blame me? It ain't every day you win a few thousand dollars."

Marcus looks at him with a twisted sneer on his face. "A few thousand, huh? I thought for sure someone like you would think it's more like a few *million*." With that said, he gets up and walks toward the bar.

"Fucking prick," I say, looking at my dad.

"Now, son, what have I always told you?" he asks, but he's smiling so I know he's not mad. Shit, he probably thought worse than what I did, he just isn't saying it out loud.

"Hm, let me think…" I pause and tap my finger on my lower lip. "Oh, I remember. That you should always respect your elders…unless they are sorry pieces of shit that deserve to be put in their place." I add the last part in with a smile on my face. Like I said, he's taught me right and wrong, it just may not be in the traditional sense. But it's the way we live and it's more honorable than most people.

He laughs and nods. "Damn right, son."

The waitress walks up to our table and asks if we're ready to order. Since we already knew what we wanted before we even got here, we don't even need to look at the menu. I order a twelve-ounce T-bone steak with a side of mashed potatoes and Dad orders a New York Strip steak and a baked potato. We both decline the salad. Salads are for girls and pussies. Real men eat meat.

"So tell me again what you want to do after graduating? Do you have an idea where you want to go?" he asks after the waitress refills our sodas and walks away.

Since I was a teenager, I always knew I wanted to leave this place, but I never really knew where I wanted to go. I just thought that maybe I'd tour the US for a while and settle wherever seemed right. Now though, I know exactly where I want to go.

"I was thinking we could take a little detour down to Florida, check out the beaches on the east coast, and then head west until we reach the beach in California."

"California, huh? Why there?" he asks, genuinely interested. That's another thing I love about my dad—he's always interested in what I think, even if he doesn't understand it.

"Well, I've done a lot of research about fighting professionally and California seems to be the place that always pops up. They've got some amazing trainers out there and it seems like all the big names come from California. So I figure if I want to make it in the business, that's where I should go. You've got to learn from the best to be the best, right?"

He's quiet for a few minutes, thinking about what I said.

"What about the Marines?" he asks, though I know he isn't trying to push me to do something I may not want to do. He knows that was something I have been interested in, but wasn't really sure if it was for me. When I was little, I would always dress up in his old uniforms and play Rambo. Since I was probably five years old, that's what I wanted to be when I grew up—a soldier, just like my dad. But now, I'm not sure if that's what is meant for me. I mean, it still interests me, but I think fighting is the best bet. At least for now.

"I'm not sure, Dad. I mean, it's still a possibility, but I want to see where this takes me first. I figure I could fight for a few years and then re-evaluate where I'm at. Maybe fighting isn't for me, but maybe being a Marine isn't, either. How will I ever know if I don't try?"

I wait for him to think about what I just said and hope that he agrees with me. He always told me to never let anyone dictate my life and to always do what was best for me, what I wanted to do. He'd say I could be anything I wanted to be, and I believe him. But I still want his approval and support. I suspect I'll always want that, even when I'm old and grey.

He stares at me for a few moments, then he looks

down at the table. "I'm proud of you, son. I'm sorry I don't say that enough, but I am. I know life hasn't always been easy on you and life can be so hard that sometimes you just want to quit, but you never did—and you never will. I wish I could go back in time and do a few things different so I could have given you a better life and I wish I could have stopped your mother from leaving us. But we can't go back and change the past. We can only move forward and pray we've learned something. So no matter what you choose to do, I'll be right there with you—to guide you when you are uncertain, stand beside you when you just need someone there, and I'll walk in the shadows to look after you when you can walk the road of life on your own. I may not have done a lot in my life or have a lot to show for it, but I do have you. You are my one amazing thing in the world and I'm so damn proud to call you my son."

Listening to him talk has me almost choked up. My dad has always told me he loves me and that he's there for me and that's something a son always wants from his father. But hearing those words—that he's proud of me—does something inside of me. I don't know if I want to cry or laugh.

The waitress saves me from having to choose when she delivers our food. "Can I get you gentlemen anything else?"

My dad shakes his head and smiles at her, then she walks away.

Still a little flustered, I just stare at my plate. I feel like I should say something, anything, after what he just said, but I have no idea what. I have a billion things rolling around in my head but none of them seem to add up to how I feel.

"It ain't going to eat itself. Dig in," he says, then he follows his own advice.

Deciding that my words can wait for another day when I don't feel so raw, I shake my head and do just as he says.

My steak is cooked perfectly. I practically inhale everything on my plate. It's not often I get a meal like this and I feel like if I don't finish it fast, it could all get taken away. I've felt that way about a lot of things in my life—that they are too good to be true and it will never last. Most of the time, I'm right. But not this time.

I finish my meal before my dad, but he's close behind me.

"Damn, that was good. How was your steak, son?"

Leaning back in my seat, I pat my stomach. "Fucking delicious."

We are both quiet while we digest the good food and wait for the check. I start to think about what I should do tonight. I know there are parties going on because there are parties every Friday night, but I don't think I could stand being around anyone who frequents those parties. Even with the knowledge that I'll be leaving this place behind soon and that my life is finally starting to look up for the first time in forever, I won't risk it. Knowing the fuckers that will be there, someone will say something to piss me off and I won't be able to stop myself from beating the fuckers down. Yeah, I think I'll just have dad pick me up a six pack and go find a spot to be alone and start planning for the future.

"You ready to get out of here?" he asks as he stands up.

"Yup."

My dad slaps me on the shoulder as we walk outside but he doesn't say anything. Though, he doesn't need to. This is the happiest I think I've ever seen him. And it's not just because he won the money, though that might be a part of it, but it's because he'll be able to give me the life he has always wanted to give me. Little does he know, whether he won that money or not, I'd still be happy. Things would be harder for us, sure, but as long as he was with me and we were living our dreams, it doesn't matter how long it would take us to get there as long as we get there eventually...or at least do our best trying. Enjoying the ride, that sort of thing.

"Pull into the gas station. I gotta grab a few things, then you can drop me off down the street." I don't answer and just watch him while he walks into the store. I see him grab something out of the beer cooler and then walk to the other side of the store where they have the grocery items, pharmacy stuff, and other little odds and ends. Then he makes his way up to the front to pay for everything.

As he walks outside, I see him holding a twelve pack of Bud Light and him stuffing something into his back pocket.

"All right, now remember what I said. I give this to you and you better not drive anywhere or do anything stupid, ya hear?" he says as he gets into the truck.

"Yeah, old man, I hear ya." I laugh and pull out of the parking lot.

When I park across the street from the local watering hole, he pauses before opening the door and looks back at me. "I love you, Holden." He doesn't wait for me to say anything back before he's out of the truck and walking into the bar.

I have no idea what's making him say all the things he's said tonight and there is a part of me that is a little boy again, jumping for joy at the approval from his father. Then there's the embarrassed teenage boy who can't find the right words to say back.

I sit in my truck for a few minutes and just think back on everything he's said tonight. I always knew deep down that my dad loves me and is proud of me, but hearing him say it tonight makes me want to be better—for him. He doesn't deserve a sulking boy who gets pissed off at the littlest things. Starting tonight, I'm going to be different. I'm going to be the man he's always taught me to be. From now on, if someone does something that pisses me off, I'm going to turn the other cheek and think about all the things me and my dad are going to do when we leave this place behind.

Putting the truck in drive, I head toward home to drop my truck off. Then I'll have a couple beers out by the quarry before going to bed. Tomorrow I want to tell my dad all the things I'm sorry for and how I'm going to be better. Then we can talk about the things he wants to do when we leave after graduation. I now understand that it's not all about me. It's more than just needing my dad with me on my journey, but wanting to go on a journey *with* him—together. We'll do things that we both have always wanted to do, but couldn't.

***

I wake up to the sun heating my face and my back aching. Cracking one eyelid open, I'm blinded by the sun. Closing my eye again, I try to remember where I am and why I'm outside but the last thing I remember was sitting down at the rock quarry and drinking. I must have drank more than I thought and passed out. Shit.

Sitting up slowly, I stretch and open my eyes. It hurts like a motherfucker, but it's manageable now that I know what to expect.

Looking around, I see the empty twelve pack sitting beside me and crushed beer cans littered everywhere. I usually never drink more than six, but last night they were going down so good, I must have drank the whole damn thing without even realizing it. At least I didn't get into any trouble and no one found me out here. That would be a bitch to explain where I got the alcohol and would have Dad pissed at me for a long time, let alone willing to buy me beer anytime soon.

Once I'm standing, I'm happy that I'm not hungover. I have a little bit of a headache, but that I can handle. I start picking up the cans and placing them back into the box before starting my walk home. Don't want to leave any evidence I was here.

It only takes me five minutes before I'm walking through the front door. Not really sure what time it is or what time my dad got home, I try to stay as quiet as possible, but when I walk past his open door, I see that he's not there.

I head back toward the living room. I look at the couch, thinking maybe I missed him sleeping there when I walked in, but he's not there either.

Maybe he went somewhere, but I could have sworn his bike was outside. Looking out the window to confirm it is indeed there, I decide to just wait for him. I can't wait to tell him the revelations I had last night. Not just about wanting to be a better son, but of what I want to do with my life. I thought for sure fighting was what I really wanted, but now I'm not so sure. I still don't think I want to go to the Marines right away, but I'm keeping that option open for now. What I really want to do is travel with my dad for a while. We could tour the US and see all the places we always dreamed of seeing but never thought it'd be possible. I think California is still where I want to go, but we could move to Canada for all I care.

Heading into my room, I grab some clean clothes and jump in the shower. I think sitting under the hot spray will help ease the pain in my back from sleeping outside last night.

Once I'm done getting dressed, I walk into the living room, checking to see if Dad came home while I was in the shower, but that's a no-go. I wonder where he is. I hope he's not out looking for me. Maybe I should text him to tell him I'm home. Digging my phone out of my pocket, I shoot out a quick text.

Me: Hey old man, I'm home. Where are you?

Walking into the kitchen, I look around for something to eat but don't find much. Shit, we should have gone shopping last night. We have nothing to eat around here. Digging in my pocket, I pull out some cash I had left over from last week when Dad gave me some money for gas, so I decide to head down to the gas station for a slice of pizza or a bag of chips.

Making my way toward my truck, I see a police cruiser pull up. Not sure why they are here, I wait for them in front of my truck. Hopefully no one saw me out at the quarry last night or leaving this morning.

"Holden," Officer Jacobs says as he stops in front of me.

I can't read his face so I'll just have to tread carefully. If he's not here because of last night, then I'm not telling him.

"Officer. What can I do for you?" I try to sound relaxed and calm. He doesn't like me very much since that night a few months ago when he was trying to break up a fight and I "accidently" elbowed him in the nose. Fucker got me back by making me spend the night in jail though.

He looks down at his feet while rubbing the back of his head like whatever it is that he needs to say is painful for him. "I need you to come down to the station, son."

I feel a prickle of irritation at the word "son" when he's referring to me, but I hold my tongue. New leaf, remember?

"Sure thing. Lead the way." I go to open my truck door, but he reaches a hand out to stop me.

"I'll drive."

I let out a sigh and instead of answering him, I just follow him over to his squad car.

We don't talk the whole way to the station and I still have no idea why he's bringing me in. Usually, if he thinks I did something wrong, he would gloat and rub whatever it is in my face—whether I actually did it or not.

He parks on the side of the street right in front of the door. He gets out and waits for me to catch up to him. At least I didn't have to ride in the back of the cruiser. I feel like a caged dog when that happens. Thank God that's only happened once. Okay, maybe two or three times. Four, max.

Officer Jacobs leads me to a small office toward the back of the station. When I walk in behind him, he closes the door and sits down behind his desk.

"Please sit down, Holden. I'm afraid I have some bad news."

Wanting to get this over with as fast as possible so I can get something to eat and find my dad, I sit down and wait patiently.

"It's about your father." He pauses and rubs the back of his neck again. Before he can go on, I laugh and shake my head.

"What did the old man do? Public intox? OWI? Or wait, don't tell me, he got into a bar fight?" I laugh again, thinking about the last option. My dad is usually a mellow guy, but if you push him hard enough he's one mean sonofabitch. I've never seen him in action, but I've heard stories and have seen him lose his temper a few times with some of the neighbors. Man, I'm going to have fun giving him shit for this for a long time. He's never going to live this down.

"Well, yes, there was a fight, but—"

"Maybe I should let him sit in the tank for the day. That's what he'd do for me." I laugh again just thinking about his homecoming later tonight.

"Holden. Please, let me finish."

He waits until he sees that I'm not going to interrupt again, but that doesn't stop me from laughing on the inside.

"Like I was trying to say before. There was an altercation at the bar your father was at last night. We got a call from the bartender around one this morning. He said there was a group of men fighting in the alley and that it looked like a few of them had weapons. We got there as fast as we could, but by then the fight was already over and everyone was gone. When we went into the alley to take a closer look, we found your father." He stops again and looks down. I know my dad can handle himself in a fist fight, but knowing there were weapons, it makes me worried. How badly injured is he?

"Is he going to be all right?" I ask quietly.

He takes too long to answer, so I get up and head toward the door. Fuck it, I'll go to the hospital and find out myself.

"Holden, wait. *Holden*!" he shouts as I ignore him and make my way through the building to outside. The hospital is only about a mile away. I don't have my truck, but I can walk there. It would be faster than going home to get my truck.

Just as I get outside, I feel someone grab my arm. I yank out of the grasp and turn around. Officer Jacobs is standing there, looking a little uncertain, but determined. He has every right to be uncertain. I'll drop his ass if he keeps me from getting to my dad.

"Let me go."

I turn to go, but the next words out of Officer Jacobs' mouth stops me cold.

"Holden. He's gone, son. I'm so sorry."

I just stand there. I couldn't have heard him right. My dad isn't dead. He must mean he's not at the hospital anymore. Yeah, that's it. He's probably already home, waiting for me.

"By the time we got there it was already too late. He suffered a blow to the head, probably from a tire iron, and a gunshot wound to the chest. I'm sorry, Holden, but he's dead."

It's with those last words that every piece of thread that was holding me together snaps. No longer able to hold the beast that lies in wait at bay, I was no longer Holden, a seventeen-year-old boy. I was no longer anyone's son. I was now a man that had been wronged. A man that would do whatever it took to find the people who did this. I didn't even recognize who I was anymore, but I knew nothing would ever the same again.

CHAPTER 2

I feel a burning in my gut, like I could literally breathe fire. I don't want to believe my dad is dead, but I can feel it in my heart—or where it used to reside—that it's true. My dad was murdered.

Turning around to face Officer Jacobs, I get right in his face. "Who did it?" I say in a deadly voice that I don't even recognize. It's like something has taken over my body. I'm no longer the beast I'm used to turning into, but a demon of Hell. It's a welcome feeling. It helps hide the pain.

"Just calm down, son. Let's go back inside and we can talk about this." Five minutes ago I would have let it slide, but not now.

"I asked you a fucking question!" Deep down I know this isn't a road I should go down, but it's the only way for me now. When my father was killed, I died too, so there is no more letting things roll off my back or go in one ear and out the other. No more wanting to be nice and just make it through the next few months. What do I have to look forward to now? Not a goddamn thing. I can't turn the other cheek. Not this time.

"Holden. You're walking a very thin line right now. I understand you're upset, but you don't want to do this, I can promise you that."

Fuck this shit. I don't need him to find out who has lived their last day on this hell rock.

Turning around, I storm off down the street and head toward my house. I can hear Officer Jacobs yelling at me to stop, but it's a lost cause—*I'm* a lost cause. I couldn't care less if I go to jail. I couldn't care less if I die tonight—as long as I can take the motherfucker who took my dad away with me too, I don't care.

I make it home in fifteen minutes. I barely even remember the walk here, but I don't need to. All I need to know is that I'm getting in my truck and driving down to the bar where it all happened— where my father took his last breath.

I have enough sense not to drive like a maniac and avoid going to the bar right away. I'm sure Officer Jacobs will be looking for me there, so I head out of town and just drive for a while. As much as I try to get my anger down to a somewhat normal level and try to get a piece of myself back, it's hopeless. The fucker that killed my father not only took my dad away from me, but he took myself away from me too. I don't have it in me to care right now though and whoever did it will soon find out what a huge mistake it was to kill my father. They fucked with the wrong man.

I've felt this way a few times in my life and it's always when I'm angry and about ready to knock someone out, but this time it's different. It's worse.

It's like there's no controlling it and no going back from it. Whatever is taking over my body, mind, and soul is here to stay. Maybe that's a good thing, though. I don't want to think of the good things in life or plan for a future that doesn't include my dad.

An hour later, the only thing I've managed to do is get more pissed at what happened and more determined to find the fucker who did this. I may only be seventeen, but when he feels my wrath, it will be like he's dancing with Lucifer himself.

While I was I driving, I decided that I would do to him what he did to my dad—minus the gun. I don't have one and I know my dad didn't have one either, and it would be too hard to get one on such short notice. I'll just beat him with a tire iron. I know Officer Jacobs didn't say that was for sure what was used, but I'm just going to go with it. But I won't make it quick for him. I'll make sure to hit him where it'll hurt the worst, but not kill him quickly. I hated science and any other class that had to do with the human body, but at least I know where all the major organs are and how to hit him where he'll feel it the most.

Stopping back at home, I pack as much as I can into a bag and look around my father's room for anything I don't want to leave behind. I find his old dog tags, a picture of me and him when I was probably ten, and a few of his shirts.

While I'm digging through his dresser drawer, I find a shoe box. Not sure what's inside and if it's something that is important, I open it up. Inside are envelopes filled with hundred dollar bills. By my rough estimate, it's about thirty grand. I guess my dad put some of the money away for a rainy day. Well, it may not be raining, but I'm taking it. I know he would want me to have it, even though he may not approve why I'll be using it. But then again, maybe he would.

I don't know where the other twenty grand is or if it was stolen off his body last night, but Officer Jacobs didn't mention it so I'm just going to assume it's gone. Doesn't matter where it's at. The money I found will be more than enough to get me away from this place after I take care of a few loose ends.

Grabbing everything I'm taking with me since I won't be back, I head back out to my truck. I see my dad's Harley sitting there and decide to load it in the back as well. He taught me how to ride last year and I was planning to buy my own bike after graduation so we could go riding together. Now that will never happen, but doesn't mean that I can't take his bike to ride to remember him by. Getting it loaded is a little difficult by myself, but once I have the bike strapped down, I get in my truck and head toward downtown.

I don't want my truck to be spotted, so I park a few blocks away in an alley by a dumpster. This way I can make a quick getaway if needed, and for what I have planned, I'm for sure going to need it.

Grabbing the tire iron, I head toward the busy bar.

As I get closer, I realize the place is packed. There are about thirty cars parked in the lot and then there are about ten motorcycles parked on the street. I still have no real plan to find the person or group that was involved with killing my dad, but I figure

I'll just go in and talk to the bartender first, then see if anyone else there knows anything. I have a feeling that whoever did it will be there tonight, maybe even bragging about what they did and spending the money they probably stole. If they are, I hope they've made peace with whatever they need to because they won't be alive for much longer.

Before I head inside, I walk around the side and into the alley. Seeing a dumpster off to the side, I figure that's where my father took his last breath. Walking closer, I look for any sign he was here, but I see nothing. Glancing around, I notice a door that must lead inside the bar. Knowing I can't take my weapon of choice inside, I place it in the alley across from the door. Now all I need to do is lead the fucker that killed my dad out here and I'll have him right where I want him.

Making my way into the bar, I see that the amount of people inside is doubled, if not tripled, for the number of cars outside in the lot. This may be more difficult than I originally thought.

There are people everywhere; there isn't an empty seat at the bar, all the tables seem to be full, and there is barely any standing room. It's muggy as fuck in here, and I can barely breathe. Looking around once more, I notice the only place that isn't crowded is in the back, where it looks like about a dozen or so bikers are congregating. People seem to be giving them a wide berth, probably because they are in a biker gang. I'm surprised with the people in this town that they haven't starting running for the hills, screaming. You don't see a lot of bikers around here, at least not the serious biker types—

the ones that are in it for life and not just extracurricular purposes.

I have half a mind to start with them, thinking that if someone caused trouble last night and killed my father, it would be them. But something makes me rethink that train of thought. Instead of approaching the bikers, I head straight for the bar.

When the bartender sees me, he gets an odd look on his face and looks toward a group of three men off to the side of the bar before coming over toward me.

"You can't be here, kid. Go on home now."

I know he knows who I am, and probably why I'm here, but what he doesn't know is that I'm not leaving without what I came for. It's gonna take a whole lot more than that to make me leave.

"My father was here last night. I want to know who he was with," I say calmly.

The bartender looks back at the same group of three men as before, then turns back to me. "I don't know what you're talking about, kid, so it's best you just leave."

He looks almost sincere, but there's something in his eyes that isn't truth. Leaning in close, I give him one more chance. "Listen here, motherfucker. Someone killed my father right outside these walls and I know you know who did it. All you need to do is point them out."

The bartender hesitates for a few moments, thinking about what he should say, but I can tell he isn't going to cooperate.

"Yeah, okay. Your old man was here last night. He was drinking and trying to start shit with everyone. I tried to cut him off and told him to just go home, but he wouldn't listen. He started fighting with a group from out of town and they went outside. That's all I know. Now, you need to leave."

Why the fuck was he so desperate for me to leave? And why do I feel like he's lying? It's not just because that doesn't sound like how my dad would act, but it's something else. Maybe the way his eyes are darting back and forth between me and that small group of men watching my every move, but it's also just a feeling.

Looking over to the group of men, I stare long and hard at them. Then it clicks. These are the men that killed my father. That's why the bartender was looking at them when he saw me come in and more so when he was talking to me. It also would explain why they haven't taken their eyes off me, either.

I need to lure at least one of them outside, and I have a feeling the one that delivered the final blow to my father will be the one to follow.

Dropping my head, I pull my facial features to show nothing before looking back at the bartender. "All right. Thanks for your help." I lace my voice with sorrow and disappointment, like I believe what he told me.

"I really am sorry, kid," the bartender says just before I turn around and head toward the back. There's a door that leads out to the alley where it all started. This is where I want to lead his killer— where he will take *his* last breath.

As I walk past the bikers, I notice one of them has his eyes on me. He's older than the rest, but is younger than my father. He has darker hair, but it's cut short, and he's fucking huge. But what really makes me take notice is his eyes—they are intense but caring. It's like when I lock eyes with him, he can see inside of me and knows what I'm thinking, what I'm going through. It almost makes me stop in my tracks, but then I remember that my father is dead—he was murdered—and I'm here to get my revenge.

Steeling myself, I look away and walk out the back door. It's dark in the alley, barely any light shines from the street lights. Good. That will work in my favor.

I make my way to the opposite side of the alley and lean against the wall, my eyes burning a hole into the door that leads back inside the bar, just waiting for someone to come out. And I don't have to wait long.

The door opens and two men step outside. They are both from the group of three that the bartender kept glancing at. I fucking knew it!

When the door closes, one of the men—he's a little on the bigger side and looks to be slow moving—stands to the side of the door and crosses his arms over his chest. He's the lookout. The other man—he's tall with longer, stringy hair—walks toward me.

Stopping in the middle of the alley, he crosses his arms and smiles a cruel smile. "You looking for someone, boy?" he sneers, and I know instantly that he's the one who killed my father.

"Not anymore I'm not," I growl. My blood pumps harder now and my hands itch to plow into his face and wrap around his throat. All in due time.

I want to make him suffer first.

The man by the door laughs, which just pisses me off even more. Motherfucker will get his after I deal with this shitface.

Taking a few steps closer to me, the man in front of me snickers. "So let me get this straight. You come here tonight and what? Confront me about your piece of shit daddy? Is that it, boy?"

Hearing him even mention my father has me seeing red, but I hold back. "Nah. I came here tonight to put the motherfucker that killed my father in the ground."

Now both men are laughing like this is some kind of joke. Like that fact that they took the only person I have on this earth I care about away from me is a laughing matter.

Not being able to hold back any longer, I rush forward and catch him by surprise with a powerful uppercut to his chin. He stumbles back a little and shakes his head.

"That was the only one you'll get, boy. Now I'm going to do to you what I did to your daddy," he growls as he pulls a knife from his back pocket.

"That's what you think, fucker," I say as I reach down to grab my weapon—the tire iron.

Out of the corner of my eye, I catch movement from the door. The lookout man is moving in, but still keeping off to the sidelines, no doubt ready to step in if he thinks his friend is losing.

Focusing back on the guy I want to rip apart with my bare hands, I smile the first smile since I found out about my dad. It's cruel and full of vengeance. "Let's do this."

Everything seems to happen in slow motion after that. The man with the knife strikes out toward me, barely missing my stomach. I move out of reach, but I miscalculate his speed because before I even realize it, he slashes my arm, just above my elbow. The sting barely registers, but is enough to fuel the rage inside of me to make him pay. I'm going to peel his skin off his body slowly with his own fucking knife. I don't want to make it fast, I want to torture him.

Swinging the tire iron around wide, I clip the side of his face. It isn't hard enough to kill him or knock him out, but it was hard enough to drop him to the ground.

I see lookout guy step forward, but before he even takes two steps, the back door swings open and five of the bikers come out—the first being the older biker I noticed in the bar.

The lookout guy turns around as fast as he can, but it's not fast enough. The biker swings and it's a devastating blow to his head. He's down and out, maybe even dead. Not that I care. I'd hoped to kill him myself, but beggars can't be choosers.

The man I'm fighting looks around and notices the bikers coming closer, but I won't let them interfere. He's mine and it's time for him to pay for his sins. I lift the tire iron above my head, ready to deliver the final blow. I don't have time to make it slow and as painful as possible. But hopefully it'll be enough for me to just kill him.

Before I'm able to deliver the hit, the biker grabs my wrist to stop me.

"You sure you want to do this, son?" the biker

asks. It isn't condescending or mocking. He asks me the question like he is genuinely curious and concerned for me.

Still looking down at the man that killed my father, I can only nod. This is exactly what I want to do. I wish I could do more, but this will have to do. Instead of letting my arm go, however, he forces me to lower it.

Further enraged that he is keeping me from avenging my father, I swing my other arm out and land a solid hit to his face. Everything around me turns hazy with a red tint to it. My vision tunnels, the only thing I can focus one is the motherfucker that killed my father and the man standing in my way.

"He killed my father! Shot him point-fucking-blank and walked away like it was *nothing*. Like he didn't just take the only person I have left away from me. He needs to fucking pay for what he did. He deserves to die," I roar.

The biker straightens up and walks toward me slowly with his hands up, like he means no harm. Fuck, the way I'm feeling, I could level every single one of them. Nothing is going to stop me from taking what is rightfully mine—this man's life.

"I agree with you, son. I'm not saying he should live. But think about where you are right now. Someone could have called the cops. I'm sure they're probably looking for you anyway if your only parent was killed last night. Am I right?" the biker asks.

I try shaking my head to consider what he's saying, knowing he's probably right, but I just can't see fucking reason. The monster inside of me is snarling and begging to taste blood. Begging to take a life for a life. The only thing I can see is myself putting an end to the pain. To right a wrong.

The biker must notice that I'm not hearing him because he steps forward again, but this time, he doesn't stop until he's right in front of me. It's not menacing and he's not afraid that I'll lash out at him again.

"Look. Why don't you let my brothers over there take this piece of shit to one of our warehouses?" he says as he points to the man I hate more than anything. "You and I will meet them there after we have a talk. I promise you, he will pay for what he did and what pain he caused you—either by your hands or ours. But let's have a chat first, yeah?"

I know he's right. I know this isn't the place to do this and he's right about the cops probably looking for me. Fuck!

Afraid that if I speak the barely suppressed violence will take over again, I just nod. The biker nods toward the others and they all move forward like an army of one and drag the man toward the other side of the alley. He screams and flails around until one of the bikers kicks him in the stomach and slams his head into his knee, knocking him out cold.

Once they're out of sight, the biker in front of me pulls my attention back to him. "Did you drive here?"

Nodding again, I start walking toward my truck, not even looking to see if he's following me. When I reach my truck, I open the door and wait until he gets in with me.

"Name's Mack," he says as I start the truck.

"Holden," I clip out.

"Okay, Holden. Why don't you tell me a little more about you and what's going on? If I'm going to help you, I need to know what we're working with."

"I never asked you to fucking help me. I was doing just fine on my own," I yell, angry he thinks I need his help. Angry my father is dead. And angry that the man who killed him is still breathing, no matter if it's only delayed a few minutes. Every minute he's alive when my father is dead is too long.

"I know you didn't, son, but what do you think killing that man is going to solve? I know he did you wrong and took your dad away from you, but what happens to you once he's dealt with? How old are you? Are you still in school? Do you have a job or a place to go after? What if you get caught? These are the things you need to think about. These are the things I can help you with if you let me."

My rage starts to simmer, but only enough for me to finally hear what he's saying. Like my dad has done my whole life, Mack is just trying to look out for me—trying to make sure I think before I act.

I give him the only answer I can.

"My dad was my best friend, all I had left, and the only person who cared about me. We were going to move right after I graduated next month. He had just found out he won the lottery last night and everything was looking up for us. We were going to be okay. But now he's gone and I have no one, so it doesn't matter what happens to me. My father is dead and I have no one else and nowhere to go. That man took my father's life. It's only fair I get to take his."

It's probably not what he wanted to hear, but it is what it is.

Mack is quiet for a few minutes, thinking about what I said, before he finally speaks. "I know the pain and rage you are feeling, son, but you have to let it go. If you let it, it will eat you alive. When I saw you in that bar, it was like I was looking into the eyes of Lucifer himself. This isn't the road I want you to take—killing a man changes you. But I also understand the feeling of being wronged and having something so priceless taken away from you." He pauses again, making sure I'm listening. "I'll make you a deal. You say you only have a month left of school and I'm here on club business for another month. You finish your schooling, because I have a feeling that's what your father would have wanted. I'll hold the fucker that killed your dad, keep him alive until after you graduate. Then, you can decide if this is the road you want to take. But regardless of what you decide to do with him, I want you to consider something else. My brothers and I are from California and a part of a club—a family, if you will. I want you to consider coming back with us when this is all said and done. You don't have to join our club if you don't want to, though I noticed that you have a nice-looking bike back there. You can still have people in your life that care about you, son—we can be that for you. So think about coming back with me and joining our brotherhood, but for right now, what do you say about waiting to make any life-altering decisions until after you graduate? Okay?"

Everything Mack said was right on. My father would want me to finish school first. And even though I want to end this right here, right now, I know that this is the best thing to do. Having someone talk to me the way Mack just did, like he cares about what happens to me and is trying to help me, I know I'd be stupid to walk away from that. I don't know if I'll take him up on following them back to California or joining their motorcycle club, but I do know that it'd be nice to be a part of something bigger than myself. Or just to be a part of anything again.

Looking at him, I hold out my hand to him to shake. "You have a deal, though I can't promise that I'll make the decisions you think I should make. I can promise I'll hold off until after graduation to make them, though."

With that, I put the truck in drive and think about everything Mack just offered. Maybe things won't turn out so bad after all. And even though I still can't feel any old piece of myself, I can still feel the monster…but maybe it's not the end of the world.

CHAPTER 3

Age 26

Lying in bed at the clubhouse with my eyes closed, I try to shut my mind off. I know I've barely slept, as well as I know that as soon as I open my eyes, I'll see the clock flash that it's three a.m. It's the same thing every fucking morning. I swear that night at the bar when Mack said he could see Lucifer in my eyes, he cursed me because not only is that where I got my road name—Louie, short for Lucifer—but I swear it's why I am always awake at this hour. Three a.m., the devil's hour.

Thinking about that night brings all those feelings of rage back tenfold, although I'm able to control it better now. After taking Mack back to the house I had shared with my dad my whole life, we sat down and figured out how the next month of my life would go.

Mack stayed with me at my house for that month. While I was at school, he did whatever it was that he was there for–club business, he'd said. I never did find out what that was, but I guess I never really asked, either. I had too much on my mind.

When I'd get home from school, Mack would already be there. Even on the days that I said "fuck it" and left school early, it was like he knew and would always be waiting for me.

He'd ask me how my day was, made sure I did what little homework I had to do to graduate, and cooked a hot meal before I went to my room. And it was always something better than ramen, though sometimes I wished for that because it reminded me of my dad.

At times, I hated Mack for keeping me from doing what I originally sought out to do that night. I hated that he called the police station to tell them that he was my guardian. And he spoke to the school I attended and told them that he was my uncle and to call him if there were any problems. I learned that when the first day I went back to school when I got into a fight with some punk who was talking shit about my dad, saying that he deserved what he got.

Mack showed up, but instead of scolding me for fighting, he pulled me aside and told me that fighting shouldn't be the answer to every problem— that there was a time and place for it—he told me there are extenuating circumstances, that every man had to man up and never back down. This just happened to be one of those times. Honor and respect. He told me that he was proud I stood up for what I believed in and who I cared about. It was never wrong to stand up for family. He taught me that. No matter what the reason, if it involves your family, whether they are blood or not, you fight.

After that day, no one bothered me or even spoke to me, which was good. I just needed to get through that month. I knew I was going to leave that town soon; I just didn't know where I was going to go. Did I take Mack up on his offer and follow him to California? Shit, that's where I wanted to go when my dad was still alive, anyway. But sometimes when I thought about it, it felt wrong to go there with him. That was our plan, and without him, it just didn't seem right to go if he wasn't going to be there too. I figured I would wait until the time came to make that decision. I just wanted to take one day at a time.

Then, finally, graduation came. Mack and a few of his biker brothers showed up to show support, but I was too clouded with rage and, I can admit now, sadness over my father's death. Mack wanted to take me out to eat to celebrate, but I didn't want anything to do with that. I just wanted him to take me to where he was holding the man that stole my dad from me. Clyde was his name.

Mack never once told me where they were holding Clyde, fearing that I would sneak out and kill him before I graduated. I probably would have done that too if I'd known where he was. Though maybe a part of me would have held me back. My dad always taught me to honor and keep my word. It would have been like spitting on his non-existent grave to go back on what I told Mack.

So when Mack started driving toward my house, I instantly became angry, thinking he wasn't going to hold up his end of the deal.

I started yelling at him and told him to pull over. I'm not proud of this, but when he did, I wanted to kill him. Here I did everything he asked me to do, upheld every part of my end, was honorable, but he was keeping me from doing what was promised to me. What was my right to see through to the very end.

When we both got out and he met me in the front of the truck, I swung. I started screaming at him and hitting him over and over. But let me tell you this, Mack is one tough sonofabitch. He never once wavered, never once lashed out, and never once yelled back. He just let me pound on him, let me blame him for everything and everyone that wronged me.

When I was exhausted and completely drained, he just stood there and waited. And when I finally calmed down, he took me in a hug and told me that he was there for me and that everything would be all right. Then he released me and got back in the truck and waited for me to follow.

Back on the road again, he drove us two blocks away from my house to what looked to be an abandoned house. I followed him inside and down into the basement. There, sitting chained to the wall, was the man that killed my father.

Shaking the thoughts from my head, I open my eyes and see that it's 3:03 in the morning. Knowing I won't get any more sleep, I get up and head downstairs to the kitchen to start some coffee. Today is going to be a long-ass day.

***

Two hours later, I've had a full workout in the club gym and have had more coffee than I can stand. Not able to be here with my thoughts any longer, I decide to head into the shop and get some sketching done. I only have a few appointments today, but I do have a client that wants to add to his back piece, so I can start working on that for him.

When I step outside, I see Mack standing by my bike. Not sure why he's out there waiting for me, I head over.

"I thought old men like you needed their beauty sleep," I say as a way of greeting.

There's something on his mind, though I can't tell if it's club business or not, but I know it's not going to be something I like.

"Just spit it out already," I say without looking at him. I just want to get this over with so I can get to the shop. I'm itching to get away and hole up in my room at Sinners Ink. Tattooing has turned into a form of therapy for me. I feel calmer when I'm sketching or when I have that tattoo gun on someone's skin.

Letting out a long sigh, he turns toward me.

I don't know how he does it, but with that one sigh I feel like I've disappointed him or let him down. I have a feeling I know why he's out here waiting for me. Things have been really tense the last few years, more so than usual. With the whole Dani and me thing, then Blaze coming around and finding out that him and Dani had a thing, then her getting kidnapped, then everything that went down with Harlow and me, Toby falling in love with Sara and the whirlwind of her past coming back to bite us all in the ass, Dani's pregnancy scare and then the twins. Add that all on top of the fact that I can't stop thinking about Harlow or wondering if she'll ever come back—I've been an ass lately—snapping at my brothers, quick to using my fists to solve everything, and letting things slip past me.

In the last two months, I've felt the monster inside start to take over. Maybe even more than when my father was murdered. Everything is falling apart, including me. I'm actually surprised he's waited this long to call me out. I need to get my shit together, if not for me and my club, then for the man that took me in and treated me like his own flesh and blood.

"Sometimes I feel like I failed you, Holden." Hearing my given name, I'm instantly on alert and know I've fucked up. Mack hasn't called me by my real name since before I patched into the club. After I walked into that basement, my fate was sealed and my name was always Louie to anyone that mattered, though only Mack knows why or how I got that name.

I don't know how to respond to his comment so I just wait him out. Maybe I should tell him I'm sorry and that I'll do better, that I won't let him down again. But I don't. I stay quiet because I have no idea where he's going with this conversation or how he thinks he failed me, but I don't need to wait long.

"Maybe I was wrong. I never should have made that deal with you. I should have just told you that I would take care of it and been there for you. I don't

41

regret asking you to come back with me or you joining the club, but maybe I should have done more to shelter you. You were so young. You never should have been faced with what you had to face or choose to take someone's life or not. Now, every day, I watch you drown in your pain and anger. I know you have trouble sleeping—I don't know if it's nightmares or what, but I know you struggle. And I guess I just feel that there was something I could have done different to make your life better."

Hearing the pain and regret in his voice guts me. After Mack took me in that basement and watched me torture and kill Clyde, we never once talked about that night—not like I probably would have, anyway.

Then, the next morning, I woke up and knew I had to go with him. It felt right packing up what little I had and following Mack to California. And I haven't regretted that decision once. I don't even regret taking that man's life, he deserved what he got. But maybe we should have talked before now. I hate that Mack feels this way. He was like a second father to me, he was always there when I needed him.

Taking a deep breath before letting it out, I turn to face him. "I know we've never really talked about it and I never said anything, but I appreciate everything you have done for me—including giving me the choice and chance to do what I needed to do. Do I have trouble sleeping? Yes. I'm not gonna lie, but it has nothing to do with what I did or the deal you made with me. I don't have nightmares and I don't regret anything—especially not following you back here or joining the club. I don't know why I don't sleep right, but I want you to know, it's not because of anything you did or didn't do."

I take a break to catch my breath and gather the rest of my thoughts. It's not easy talking about this, but I know Mack needs to hear it, maybe as much as I need to say it.

Mack opens his mouth to say something, but I can't let him—not yet. Holding up my hand, I motion for him to stop. "Just let me finish. I need to get this out."

I wait until he nods.

"I never had a lot in my life. I had my dad and the things we used to do together—or more of what we talked about doing together, but they were good memories all the same. Granted, not all of them were good, but I thank God every day that I had him in my life for eighteen years. I wish I had even one more day with him, but that's not the hand that was dealt to me, and I understand that and am as okay with it as I can be. But the things you did for me—I gotta tell you, man, those are things I am truly thankful for. You didn't have to stop me from killing that fucker in the alley. You didn't have to listen to a pissed off, vengeful teen. And you sure as fuck didn't have to stick around and make sure I didn't fuck my life up. But you did. You gave me something to look forward to, something to work toward. Sure, it's not what most people would do, but it was exactly what I needed. It's not about right or wrong in others' eyes, it's about what you did right for *me*. I'll admit, I still think about that night and the things I did to that guy, but I will never regret it or think poorly of what you offered. Never. So, I guess what I'm trying to say is this—I'm good. I may have problems, but who the fuck doesn't these days? I'm alive, I'm living the life I want, and I'm surrounded by those that would lay their life down for me and vice versa. I don't say it enough, but I love you, man. Thank you for everything you've done for me. For being there when you didn't have to be."

He's not looking at me, but I can tell my words have struck a chord with him—they hit him deep. We aren't ones to voice our feelings a lot, but when we do, that shit's deep.

Finally, Mack composes himself enough to look at me and speak.

"I hear ya. I'm not saying that I still think it's okay or that I didn't fuck up, but as long as you're all right, that's all I can ask for. You let me know if you ever need to talk though, don't hold that shit inside, ya hear? I don't ever want to see that look in your eye like I did that night. It's come close a few times and I see it getting close now, so if you need something or need to talk, find me. I don't care where I am or what I'm doing."

I just nod and slap him on the back. "I hear ya. Now go back to bed, ya old bastard." I end on a laugh, and duck when he moves to slap me upside the head.

As he walks back inside, I can hear him mumble something that sounds like "fucker."

Getting on my bike, I take a deep breath and let it all out. I actually feel pretty good after that talk with Mack. Granted, if anyone finds out about our heart to heart, we'll both never hear the end of the pussy jokes, but I'm glad we finally cleared the air. We should have done that a long time ago.

On the drive to the shop, I think about that night one more time to try and make peace with what happened and what I did—put it all behind me once and for all. I think about seeing the man that killed my dad chained and gagged in that basement. I think of the rage and demonic out of body experience I had. I think about all the things I did to him to force him to feel physically half the pain I felt emotionally from the loss of my father. I think about how he begged for his life and wondered if my father pleaded for his life too. And I think about what I felt when I finally ended his sorry excuse for a life.

I still feel like it wasn't actually me that did all of those things—even though I know it was and I'm fucking happy that I did, don't get me wrong. But from the moment I found out about my dad's death, it was like I was no longer me, I was no longer Holden. And I suppose that's the truth in a sense. Holden died the same night my father did, and in his is place Louie was born. I may not be what others think of as righteous or even good man, but I know deep down in my black soul that my father is looking down on me and is proud of the man I've become. And I'm happy with the man I'm become…mostly.

Pulling up outside of Sinners Ink, I feel better than I have in a long time. I feel free. There are still things missing and things that piss me off, but I feel good.

I park my bike and take my key out to unlock the door, but as I get ready to insert it, I see someone inside, sitting at the front desk. What the fuck?

Pulling my pistol out from behind my back, I quietly open the door. Once I'm inside, I point my gun at the intruder, then close and lock the door behind me. The noise alerts the guy to my presence, but there's nowhere for him to go. He's a fucking dead man.

"Who the fuck are you and what are you doing here?" I ask in a voice that leaves no room for questions.

He doesn't try to move or answer me. Losing all patience, I walk closer. The motherfucker better start talking soon before I just decide to shoot him instead of giving him a chance to explain himself.

I make it halfway across the room before the guy finally snaps out of it and tries to get up and flee. I take two quick steps to cut him off, but he just as quickly turns to move the other way. I reach out and wrap my arm around his throat and hold the gun to his head. Being this close to him, I notice how small he is. He's just a fucking kid!

"I'm only gonna ask you one more time. Kid or not, I'll put a fucking bullet in you. Who the fuck are you and what do you want?" I growl.

I don't expect the answer I get. "It's me, Louie." I'm so shocked that I instantly drop my arms and step back.

It can't be.

I must be fucking hallucinating, but then she turns around and I can see her face. Either both my eyes and ears are deceiving me, or it's really her.

"Harlow?"

CHAPTER 4

Harlow

Being back in this shop and staring at Louie again after two years away has me thinking two different things at the same time—why the fuck did I come back and why the fuck didn't I come back sooner? They are both playing front and center in my mind and I have no idea which one will win in the end. Was it a mistake to be gone this long or was it a mistake to come back?

For the past two years, I have been drifting. I've been nowhere and everywhere at the same time and I'm so fucking tired. Tired of running, tired of the pain, tired of the anger, but mostly, I think I'm tired of being lonely. But at the same time, I'm not ready to let anyone else in, either. Letting people in only opens the door to more pain.

I honestly don't even know why I came back. Though I guess when I really think about where I've been, it's like my subconscious always knew where I'd end up. It's like it has been driving me here from the very start—starting in North Carolina, heading down to Florida, Georgia, Louisiana, Texas, Oklahoma, Kansas, Nevada, and now California. I've actually only been about two hours away from here for the past few months. I knew it, but I guess I just wasn't ready to face what I left behind. I'm still not, so what the fuck am I doing?

"Harlow? Is that you?" Louie asks in disbelief, like he can't even fathom that I'd come back, like he doesn't think I belong here.

"No, it's the fucking tooth fairy," I say, deadpan.

Fuck, why did I think coming back here would be a good idea? Oh wait, I didn't. No, that was my fucked up brain telling me to come here, and for what? To be questioned and judged? I don't think so.

Turning around on my heel, I head for the door, but only make it a few steps before Louie grabs me by the arm. It's tight enough that I can feel just a small bite of pain, but it's not bruising.

"Where the fuck do you think you're going, huh?" Louie growls angrily.

I turn around sharply while ripping my arm free at the same time. "I'm leaving. What does it look like I'm doing?"

"You're not going any-fucking-where!" he roars.

Before I can respond, I hear the bell over the shop door ring. Louie and I both turn around to and see Dani standing there, staring at us both in shock.

After a few silent moments, she whispers in disbelief, "Harlow?"

Not again. Ugh, is it really that big of a shocker that I'm here? I mean, really! So what if I've been gone for two years without calling or even so much as writing? That doesn't mean that I wasn't ever planning on coming back. Well, that might be a half-lie.

When she realizes I'm not going to answer her, or maybe she didn't want me to answer anyway, Dani rushes toward me and takes me in her arms in a tight hug.

"Oh my God. Harlow! I've missed you so much. Where have you been? When did you get back? Are you okay?" she fires question after question. If it were any other situation, I would laugh at the comical look on her face and the way her eyes are almost popping out of her head.

Letting out a deep breath, I reply, "I just got into town about a half hour ago. I still had my key from when I worked here, so I thought I'd stop by to say hi before I left town again. But if I would have known dumbass over there was going to manhandle me, I wouldn't have even bothered." I sneer toward Louie.

"The fuck you say?" Louie bristles.

"Are you deaf or just stupid? I said I stopped by—" but I don't get anything else out before Louie interrupts me.

"I heard what you said the first time. But you are sadly fucking mistaken if you think you're leaving," he says in a voice that should warn me against arguing further, but what can I say? I have no filter and my give-a-damn button is broken.

"So stupid it is then. Well, Mr. You're Not Going Anywhere, I've got news for you. Last time I checked, you ain't my daddy and you ain't my old man, so I don't know where you come off thinking you can tell me what to do, but you're dead wrong."

Louie closes the few steps that separate us and is in my face before I can even blink. "I dare you to say that again. Go on, Low, say it. Tell me again I'm not your daddy 'cause I'd love to put you across my knee and tan your ass."

Having him this close to me again after all this time has my heart beating so loud I'd be surprised if he couldn't hear it. Needing some space I try to back away, but for every step I take backwards he takes one forward.

Dani, bless her fucking heart, must sense that I'm almost to my breaking point with Louie, because she steps forward and pulls his attention off of me and onto her. "Zane is outside getting the kids out of the truck. Go out and help him for me."

I almost don't catch it when she says *kids*. What the fuck does she mean, kids? I know when I left she was pregnant, but did they have another baby while I was gone?

I'm suddenly overwhelmed with sadness thinking about it. Dani and I were becoming really good friends, like sisters almost, before I left. Feeling the gap between us now makes it seem like I'm staring across at her and all her perfection and happiness from the other side of the Grand fucking Canyon.

Louie doesn't take his eyes off of me, but he does take a step back. Thank God!

Then, after a few tense moments of our stare off, he finally turns toward Dani. "Yeah, sis, I'll go help with the rugrats," he says before looking back and pointing at me. "But we ain't done here and you ain't leaving." He doesn't give me any time to comment before he's out of the shop within seconds.

"Damn, girl, I thought you had his panties in a twist before you left, or fuck, even *after* you left he was a mess. But now. Shit, girl, he's off the rocker completely." She ends on a laugh, but I don't see how she can think this is funny. I'm feeling completely fucked up the ass where Louie is concerned.

There's no time for me to even come up with a response to what Dani just said before the door to the shop opens and two small children come barreling into the shop. Louie isn't far behind— chasing them, playfully yelling at them, picking them up and tickling them. The children, who I can tell just by their looks belong to Dani and Blaze, are laughing and loving every minute of Louie's attention. Watching him with these children almost softens me up enough to break out into a small smile, but it never comes. *You're broken, remember? Broken girls can't smile or feel happiness.*

Coming in more leisurely behind Louie, is Blaze. He has a huge smile on his face watching his children playing around and laughing. Even though it's been years since I last saw Blaze, I can notice a difference in him. He's not as hard, it seems. Before, he was always scowling or seeming pissed off about something. Dani and he were fighting more often than not. But looking at him now, he looks younger, happier. It's a good look on him.

Actually, come to think of it, Dani seems different as well. She seems to have had the same changes as Blaze; she doesn't look as hard or pissed at the world all the time now. People say that having kids ages you, but she looks younger too, just like her man. She doesn't seem like she's got a shield up anymore, as if she's waiting for something bad to happen. I'm glad she's happy and things seem to be going good for her now. If anyone deserves happiness, it's Dani. She's been through hell. It's about time she's got her piece of heaven. I just wish I could have a little slice as well. Too bad that will never happen.

Louie has changed since I last saw him too, though not the same ways as Dani and Blaze. He's harder and more guarded than he was before, which is saying something. Louie was always rough around the edges, and had this hardness that seemed almost demonic at times. But now...now there is only anger inside him. His shoulders are stiff and he has this coldness in his eyes. I don't know if this is just the way he is now, or if it's because of me, but going by what Dani said just a few moments ago, this is how it's been for a while now. Since I left. Too bad I can't find it in myself to care. Not as much as I probably should, anyway.

"Well, Harlow and I have a lot to catch up on. We'll be in my office," Dani says as she grabs my arm and hauls me off behind her. I catch a warning look from Louie, but I'm not really sure what he's warning me about. Not to leave again? Well, he can kiss my ass. I'll leave if I want to, but I do really want to catch up with Dani, at least on her life since

I've left. I don't want to get into anything that I've been doing since then. I don't want to talk about the pain. The anger. Where I've been all this time.

Once we're in her office, she sits right down and waits till I'm sitting before she starts right in with telling me about what I've missed. Everything from her pregnancy, the birth, milestones from her kids, things about her and Blaze, and how Toby is now married. That is actually a little hard for me to believe. I mean, I knew Dani was pregnant when I left, so her telling me about that isn't much of a surprise, although her having twins caught me a little off guard. But Toby married? Never thought that would happen.

After she's done filling me in on all I missed, she sits there and just stares at me, probably waiting for me to tell her about me and what I've been up to. When I don't say anything for a few minutes, Dani sighs.

"I won't make you tell me where you were or why you haven't called or anything in two years. I won't ask what happened, but I will ask this. Are you leaving again or are you going to stick around?" Dani says.

It shouldn't surprise me how forward she is, but it does. I've been away from Dani way too long and need to work back into the fact that she's not afraid to say what she thinks. Though I am happy she isn't going to push me, I have no idea how to answer her one question. Am I sticking around?

Dani must see my indecision, because she asks, "Why *did* you come back, Low? I mean, it's not like I'm unhappy about it, but you seem like you want to run out of here right this second and never look back. So it just makes me wonder...why come back in the first place?"

And that, my friends, is the question of the hour. Why come back? Knowing I owe her something, I decide to just tell her the truth.

"I honestly have no idea why I'm back, Dani. I don't even know if I made the conscious decision to make my way back here, it just sort of happened," I whisper, feeling more confused now than ever.

I figured I would come back at some point in time after I left, but once I got where I was going and found out what called me back home, I just sort of lost myself and everything I once thought was just thrown in the trash. I no longer cared about anything, even myself. I became a drifter, going from one town to the next, just trying to stay afloat as much as possible.

"I don't know what I'm doing anymore, Dani. I know deep down this is where I belong, this is my home, but at the same time, it's like there's this voice inside my head telling me that I should run and never looks back." I don't even realize I've said those words out loud until I feel Dani sit beside me and pull me into a hug.

"This *is* your home, Harlow, and you *do* belong here. I don't know what happened, but I'm here for you. We're *all* here for you," she says as she holds me, rocking me back and I start to feel angry again. Angry at her and this perfect life she has. Angry that she thinks this is my home and they are there for me. But I don't need them. None of them.

***

It's been two weeks since I've been back and every day is worse than the last. I feel like I'm a caged animal, like my skin is itching and I can't shake it. No matter where I'm at, who is with me, I feel alone and crowded at the same time. I can't stand it! I just want to call a cab and get the fuck outta Dodge, but somehow Dani convinced me to stay. At least for a little while.

I've been staying in the apartment above the shop again, but it no longer feels like home. It feels like a prison cell.

Everyone has been good to me since I've been back—too good. Dani seems to pick our friendship up where we left it before my life was shattered. Louie has tried to pick our friendship up, but there's this hidden anger toward me with him too. Blaze barely notices me, but that's nothing new. Toby is too consumed with his new wife, who seems shy and unsure around me, not like I blame her. I can tell that Sara and I would have been good friends if I would have met her before I got the life changing news and left. She's quiet, but she also has this inner fire to her. Kind of like Dani did, but it's not as subtle or as intense as Dani's. And Mack and the other guys in the club have tried to talk to me, ask how I'm doing, and include me in things, but it seems forced. Or maybe it's me that is feeling forced.

It's so strange. Deep down, I know I care about these people. But since I've been back, I feel this deep-seated hatred and jealousy toward them. They have everything I want but don't have. And will *never* have. Sure, they say they love me and that I'm their family, but I'm not. My family, my blood family, is gone. I have nothing and no one. I have me, that's it. And sometimes, I don't even feel like I have that. It's fucked up and the joke's on me.

Everything and everyone is getting to me. I hate how Louie hovers, I hate how everyone pretends like nothing happened, I hate how close everyone is, but I especially hate how much I hate myself and the life I have. I just wish it would all go away. I just want to fade into the background and not be anywhere anymore.

The bell over the shop door brings me out of my thoughts. I've been working a few hours here and there at the shop, doing my old job, but I have to share my hours and duties with Sara. It bothers me more than I know it should, but it's like I've been replaced by Sara. And I hate her for it.

"Hey, Low, how are you doing?" Sara asks in her happy, sing-song voice. How the fuck can anyone be that happy? I mean, really.

"Fine," I say, hoping she moves the fuck on fast instead of trying to talk to me more.

"Okay then, well, good. Maybe I won't have such a busy night then and I can get that inventory done for Dani," she says with a smile.

Her statement has me looking up at her in confusion. "You're here to work?" I ask in an angry voice, though I do try to hide it. Okay, that's a lie. I don't care if she sees it.

Why can't she just back off now that I'm back? I mean, it's not like she really needs to work since she has Toby to take care of her. Me, I have no one to spend my spare time with or a man to support me. Not like I'd want that, but still. She has everything, while I have nothing. Zilch. Zero. Diddly-fucking-squat.

"Oh, ah, yeah, I thought it was my night to work," she starts, and by the ongoing look of anger on my face, she starts to back up and stutter. "B-but, ah, i-if you would r-rather work it, t-that's, I'm mean, I'm g-good with that. I can just go home."

Standing up too fast that the chair practically slams into the wall behind me, I grab my things. "Forget it. I'll just grab my shit and be gone," I say with venom that shouldn't be directed at her, but it is. And she can sense it considering she looks like she could cry.

If I had a heart, I'd care that I hurt her feelings. But it's dead. Like everything else in my life.

Just then, Louie walks in the room and takes one look at Sara and rushes over. "Sar-Bear, you all right? What happened?" he asks, crouching a little so he can look her in the eyes, then glances over at me with a look of anger of his own.

"We got a problem here?" he grits out.

I don't wait for Sara to comment, I just stand up and grab my things. "Nope, no problem, boss. Sara here is my replacement; in *all* areas, it seems."

I hear Sara's breath hitch and can practically feel the anger and frustration coming off of Louie in waves, but I ignore it all and walk right out the front door. No sense in going up to the apartment, it's not mine anyway. It was once Dani's before she found purpose and people to love her and take care of her.

Then it was Sara's, until she found the same thing. But it was never mine, and never will be.

Hailing a cab, I jump in and tell the driver to just drive, but don't miss seeing Louie out of the corner of my eye storm out of the shop and rush over to the cab right before we drive away.

I should just have him take me to the nearest bus station or drive until he's out of gas, but I know I won't do that. What can I say, I'm a glutton for punishment. I live for the pain, it seems. Not like there is anything else in this life to live for. At least being here, I can make people feel *some* of the pain and anger I feel daily. It's the little things, right?

CHAPTER 5

Louie

I have no idea what is going through Harlow's fucking head anymore. Sometimes, it seems like she's her old self again, smiling and talking with Dani and I, and then it's like someone hits a switch and she turns into this raging bitch who couldn't care less about the people around her. The people who fucking care about her, who are there for her if she would just give us the chance, if she would just talk to us and tell us what happened to her. We all know something happened, there was a reason why she left in the first place, but there's more.

And that shit that she just pulled with Sara is whacked. She's fucking lucky Toby wasn't here to see how Harlow just treated her. Granted, I know she must feel weird around Sara, not knowing her and all, and I'm sure it's an adjustment to be back and have to share a job that was solely hers in the first place, but what the hell does she expect? She's the one that fucking up and left without so much as a "fuck you" or "kiss my ass." Doesn't she know that if she would have just told us why she had to leave or what was going on, that we would have stood beside her every step of the way? That we would have helped her?

"Did I do something wrong?" Sara whispers almost to herself.

Walking up to her, I pull her into a hug. She's been through so much, she's been hurt so badly, and it kills me to know that I was one of the people who did that to her. I may not have been the worst or the main cause of her pain, but I was a part of it. The things I said, how I acted, I know it cut her deep. But I'd also like to think that we've come a long way since then too. She's one of my best friends now, like a sister to me.

"No. You didn't do anything wrong. Harlow is just in a bad place right now. She's hurting and the only thing that probably makes her feel even a sliver better, is to make others feel as miserable as she does. I'm sorry she acted that way toward you, Sara, but I promise, she didn't mean it personally," I say as I hold her, hoping I'm not telling a lie.

I shouldn't promise that, especially since I have no idea what is going through Harlow's head right now, but deep down, I know Harlow doesn't mean anything by it. She really is just in pain and she's acting out. Fuck, I know that feeling better than most. I *lived* it. Breathed it for the longest time. I just need to bring her out of it, get her to talk to me, tell me what's going on or what happened. I can help her, I know I can. She just has to let me.

"Do you love her?" Sara asks as she pulls back

and looks me in the eyes with tears in hers.

Her question throws me off for a minute. *Love*? Do I love Harlow? No, I don't think so. I care about her and feel for her what I've never felt for anyone, even Dani, but I don't love her. You can't love someone who isn't around, someone who leaves you and hurts you in ways that you can't even describe.

Sara must see my thoughts painted all over my face. "I'm sorry, I shouldn't have asked that."

She tries to pull away, but instead, I pull her into one last hug. "You never have to apologize to me, Sar-Bear. It's just, before she left, things were good. Like, real good. I was starting to feel like I wasn't alone in this world anymore. I mean, I know I have the club and all my brothers, and Dani even, but sometimes, I still felt alone. But when she started working here, it was like none of that mattered, or maybe all those feelings just disappeared, I don't know. But then things got complicated, and before I could figure it out or fix it, she left. She just walked away from all of us, with just a note saying she didn't know if or when she'd be back. No explanations, no goodbyes. Just *gone*."

I think back to the way it made me feel when I saw that note. I remember thinking that it was no big deal, that maybe she just needed some time and would be back. Maybe not the next day or the next week, but she'd be back soon. But *soon* never came.

"And now she's back and instead of feeling like all is right in the world, I feel like there's still this dark hole inside me. What if what I was feeling before she left wasn't real? What if it was just a cover? And this, this feeling of darkness, is the real me? I've always been dark, and when she was here, it was like I finally had this light shined on me. I'm sure you've heard all about Dani and me, and even if you didn't, there's no need to rehash it now, but I didn't even feel that way with her. So, what if that light, that *good* feeling I had, was just a joke...a lie? I mean, if it wasn't, shouldn't I have that light back now that Harlow is here again?"

I hate having all these questions, all these unanswered what ifs or whys. I've never been the type of guy to question things or feelings. I just went with what I was feeling and let it take hold of me. But now...now I just feel lost. And angry.

Shaking my head of those thoughts, I look back at Sara. "So you asked if I loved Harlow. She's inside of me, that's for sure, but it's not love."

***

It's been a week of pure hell. Things have not gotten better with Harlow; they are getting worse it seems like every second of every day. It's feels like a race to see who the fuck is gonna snap first: me, Dani, Blaze, Toby, or Harlow. Everyone is at their breaking point. Me, because I have no idea what the fuck is going on with her and I'm pissed that she's keeping me out. She barely even fucking talks to me these days, unless it's one word answers, and even then you can tell she'd rather cut her own tongue out if it meant she wouldn't have to talk to me. And let's not forget the anger that never used to be there. She's venomous to everyone around her, even the customers. I can't figure out what happened to make her this way.

Dani, surprisingly, has been the most patient with her. I don't know if maybe Harlow has told her something, anything, for Dani to be so lenient about her actions. Shit, if you saw the way Dani was a few years ago and the way she is now, you would think that she had a twin because it's like night and fucking day. She doesn't yell or get upset with Harlow for any reason. She always says that it's okay and she just needs to get used to things or that we have to understand that she obviously went through something and we just have to give her time. Fuck that noise, I say.

Blaze, if it weren't for Dani, would have probably gone ape shit crazy on Harlow by now. But instead, Dani just tells him to take a walk or to go into her office. The past couple of days, as soon as she sees one or the other coming into the same room, she rushes Blaze out of there before either of them can say anything. She knows he's had enough. Fuck, I think she knows we've all had enough, but we don't know how to get through to Harlow. We don't know what we need to do to get the old her back, or at least have her talk to us about what's going on.

Toby was patient the first few days, but the more he saw the cold shoulder that Harlow was giving his wife, he was done. Now, whenever Harlow is in the same room with him, he just glares and then walks out. And if Sara is in the room, he makes sure that he drags her along with, though she never fights him. It's wearing her down the way Harlow is treating her, but like Dani, she thinks it will all pass and she's too fucking understanding. She said that she knows what it's like and after some time, things will go back to normal. Again, fuck that.

And then there is Harlow herself. She doesn't talk to anyone unless she has to. She snaps or barks at people, including customers, when she does talk. Sometimes, I even feel like she's baiting us to see how far she can push until we finally do snap. I don't know what she thinks will happen if she does succeed in that, though. Does she think we'll just tell her to fuck off and leave again? That we don't want her around? If that's what she thinks, she's fucked in the head. Maybe it's time for some tough love. I don't know but something has to give. And finally, the day comes when it does.

Sitting at my desk, I'm going over my schedule and list of clients and what they want done for the next week. I like to figure out what needs to be sketched out beforehand or what I need to make sure I'm prepared for each client and job.

I have a guy that wants a black panther that looks like it's climbing on his ribs, around his side, and up onto his back. Now, I'm a great fucking tattoo artist, but my style is a little different. But Dani, on the other hand, can be very versatile with every style of tattooing, so I think it may be a good idea to get her opinion and possibly even some coaching on this one. I know this guy wants it as lifelike as possible, so I need to be on my game and make sure to cover my ass on every angle.

"Dani," I yell, hoping she's not with a customer, but knowing even if she is, they won't care. Our clients are great like that. We are professional in all the areas we need to be, but we still like to keep a very, I don't know, *homey* feel to the shop. We treat all of our clients like our friends, like family. Even if that means joking around and fucking off around them. They love it, and it makes things easier on those that work here too.

A few minutes pass, and Dani still hasn't answered me, so I decide to get her here another way—pissing her off, one of my favorite things to do to her.

"Dani! Stop fucking your old man in the storage closet and get your ass over here." There, that ought to piss her off *and* get her to come here. Though, she may not be as willing to help me out now, but I'll deal. I'll just play the "clients deserve the best, so they come to the best" card with her. Gets her every time.

Not even three seconds pass before I hear her kick something and storm in my direction, cussing me out the whole way. *This is gonna be fun!*

She comes storming into my room, and the second she sees the shit-eating smile on my face, she gets even more pissed! It's a hilarious sight, but scary too. I'm man enough to admit a pissed off Dani scares me.

"What's up, buttercup?" I say in a sugar sweet voice, hoping to annoy her more. I don't know why I push her buttons, but I do. I just can't help myself sometimes.

With her face red with rage and her eyes blazing with mirth, I realize I love this girl. I love her in a way a person loves their best friend, in a way that a brother loves a sister, in a way that I never want to see her hurt but always happy. I already knew I cared about Dani, but after everything that went down between us I guess I was afraid to admit I loved her, for fear that no one would get that it was a different kind of love, myself included. But now I see the difference. You can love someone you aren't *in* love with, and that's okay.

Before she can say anything to ruin my revelation, I get up and grab her up into a crushing hug, no longer afraid to show or tell her how I feel. "I love you, Dani Girl," I say into her hair.

Instantly, I feel her deflate before she wraps her arms around me too, squeezing me tight. "I love you too," she answers back, tears evident in her voice.

"Oh, you have *got* to be fucking kidding me," I hear from the doorway.

Letting go of Dani, we both turn to see Harlow standing there, looking at us both with confusion, anger, and unmistakable pain in her eyes, but she quickly covers the hurt with contempt.

"Harlow, what are you doing here? You aren't scheduled to work today," Dani says in answer, which was the wrong thing to say, and she knows it too when she watches the rest of Harlow's sanity leave her eyes.

"Oh, I'm sorry. Did I interrupt something by showing up unexpectedly? I didn't realize I couldn't come here on my day off, but I see now why you wouldn't want me here," Harlow says to both of us, but then she directs her gaze solely on Dani. "So tell me, how does it feel to have all the brothers slaving for you?"

"Harlow, I don't know what you think is going on here, but you're wrong. And of course you can come by on your day off. What is the matter with you? Ever since you came back, you've been off your rocker," Dani says while keeping her calm. I think she's finally had enough too, or maybe this time Harlow has gone too far.

"Off my rocker, huh? Didn't know you were keeping such close tabs on me and how I've been acting. But I'm sure you have your reasons," Harlow says as she looks back and forth between me and Dani.

I step forward to put myself between the two women, knowing this is about to get outta hand and fast, but Dani puts her hand on my shoulder, stopping me. And of course, Harlow zones in on that one touch.

"Oh, I get it now. It wasn't enough that you fucked him once, you had to come back for more, am I right? Or, *maybe*, Blaze isn't giving it to you like he used to anymore. Having kids must put a huge strain on your sex life, huh? So since you aren't getting it enough from *your man*, you have to get your rocks off elsewhere, so you come to the good ol' dependable Louie. Isn't that what you called him, Dani—dependable?"

Harlow barely finishes that sentence before Dani quickly steps up to her and slaps her, hard, across the face. The force of the hit causes Harlow's face to jerk to the side, and her whole body goes with it.

Dani moved so fast I didn't even see it coming, so I'm sure Harlow was surprised as fuck. And holy shit, that slap must have hurt like a bitch, my ears are ringing from the sound of it alone.

When Harlow finally turns her face back toward us, I can see a handprint, clear as day and red as can be, on her face. And it looks like her lip was split open a little bit, because there are a few drops of blood on her bottom lip.

I feel like I need to do something, anything, to stop what's going on right now, but I'm so shocked that I just stand there and watch two of the three women I care about in my life standoff toe to toe.

The first to break the silence is Dani. "I have had enough. You walk around like the world has wronged you and that you're all alone, but you're not, Harlow. We've been here from the very beginning, but you don't get that, do you? We are *family*!"

"I don't have a family—" Harlow starts to say, but she's cut off.

"Yes you do!" Dani yells. "From the first day you started working here, you became our family and we became yours. But you walked away from us—not even telling us what happened, where you were going, and when you'd be back—*if* you'd be back. For all we knew, you fucking died, Harlow! How the hell were we to know, huh? But then you come back, and we were so fucking happy that you did. But what you're doing, the way you're acting and treating those around you, it needs to fucking stop. I've stayed quiet because I thought you'd snap out of it, or shit, at least talk to me about what's been going on. Whatever chip you have on your shoulder, share it with us. We'll help you carry it, honey. That's what family does—we will be there for you and help you walk those hard roads so you aren't alone. So, *please*, just tell us what is going on, Low. We love you and just want to be there for you."

I watched Harlow's eyes the whole time Dani said her piece, and with every word Dani spoke, it was like I was watching a little piece of Harlow leave her body, until there was nothing left. There is now nothing in her eyes—no hurt, no anger, no confusion, no love. Just nothing. She's completely broken. Void of anything that resembled the girl we once knew.

I take a step toward her to take her in my arms, but my movement snaps her out of wherever she just was. A little bit of clarity touches her eyes, and then she's gone. She turns around on her heels and runs out of the shop. But this time, I won't let her get away.

I briefly glance down at Dani to make sure she's all right. She nods. "Go get her. Bring our girl back, Louie."

She doesn't have to tell me twice. I'm out the door in two seconds and chasing after the girl that got away once before, but I won't let her run a second time. This time, she's gonna face what's happened, whatever it may be, but she'll have me this time. She'll have all of us. Because Dani was right—we're fucking *family*.

CHAPTER 6

Harlow

After running out the door, I walk at a fast pace down the street, trying not to draw unwanted attention.

I have no idea where I'm going, but I don't want to stay here. I wish I could just hail a cab and book it out of this town—out of this state, for that matter—but something inside is stopping me. As much as I want to run and never look back, I can't do that again. I won't. I know I need to face everyone here and explain, it's just harder than I thought it would be. I don't want to see the pity in their eyes or for them to say it's okay when it's not. I just need to get away for a while, even if it's only a few blocks. I want to be alone and figure out what just happened and why I reacted the way I did.

I honestly don't know what overcame me. I mean, I know Dani doesn't feel that way for Louie—she never did. It's always been Blaze for her. But seeing her in Louie's arms like that hurt. It cut me so deep that I had to cut back. I wanted them both to feel even a fraction of what I've been feeling for the past two years. Pain. Anger. Hate. But fuck, that slap across my face hurt, even though I deserved it and probably so much more.

Licking my lip, I taste blood. I figured it broke open because it stung like a bitch, and tasting the blood only confirms it.

Since I got the news two years ago, I haven't been thinking rationally about anything. Not like I've ever really made good decisions, but it's even worse now. I know that if they only knew what I was going through or what happened, that things would be different, that they could and would help me. But I'm not ready to share that with them, I don't know if I ever will be able to. Their pity would just be too much and they won't understand. Sure, they've all been dealt a shitty hand in life in their own way, but nothing like what happened to me. It's just not the same. There's no way they will be able to understand.

A few minutes later, I come up to an old playground. It looks like it hasn't seen any playtime from a child in ages. It's all rundown and broken— just like me.

Something pulls me closer and makes me stop at the swings. I feel a connection to this place, or at least to a *memory* of a place like this, but I don't want to think about that. I don't want to think about coming here with my brother or the feelings of being carefree, loved, and not alone. And I sure as shit don't want to think about how it makes me feel now that all of that is gone. I just want to sit down and forget everything, if only for a few minutes.

Taking a seat on one of the swings, I close my eyes and give myself a little push until I start to gently swing. It's peaceful sitting here alone. With the outside world shut out.

But then the memories take hold and I can picture myself years ago—as a little girl, begging to go higher. I wanted to touch the sky, but as soon as I got that extra push I needed, I was so scared, crying, begging to stop. I didn't want to fall, but there was always a voice saying, "You won't fall, Princess, I'll never let you go."

In the quiet of the night, I can almost hear it now.

"Harlow?" Hearing my name snaps me back to the here and now, where I'm once again alone. Where I feel the pain and anger and hatred.

I don't need to open my eyes to know who's here with me. It should shock me that he followed me, but deep down I think I knew he would. That I needed him to.

Louie won't let me go far, at least until we talk about what happened all those years ago, the night before my world ended. I should have pulled him aside as soon as I was back and got it out of the way, that way nothing would hold me here anymore, but I suppose I was afraid. Afraid to end whatever it is that's going on, afraid to not have anyone again, even if I don't really have him in the first place. But mostly, I think I was afraid to end the one thing holding me here. *Him*.

"Come to scold me for what I said at the shop?" I calmly ask, needing to keep the edge in my voice. I pray it will push him away, but dread it at the same time.

And there's also a part of me that knows I deserve his scolding *and* his anger. I deserve that and so much more. He should *hate* me. I *want* him to hate me. It would make this so much easier. I only wish I could convince myself that it wouldn't crush me, that I don't care if he never wanted to speak to me again after tonight. But I do.

"No."

"Then you've come to talk about what happened with us before I left?" I ask the next question with a little more heat, but also with hesitancy because as much as I know we need to talk about it, I don't want to. I just don't have it in me to fight anymore though, so I guess it's gonna happen whether I want to or not.

"Nope," he says, which makes me open my eyes to look at him.

Once he sees my eyes on his, he adds, "Not yet, anyway."

Well, at least he's honest. Just not sure what it is he *does* want to talk about. If not what happened at the shop and it's not what happened with us years ago when he took my virginity, then what?

Closing my eyes again, I ask, "Well, what is it you *do* want, then?"

He's quiet so long, that after what feels like hours, I open my eyes again and see that he's sitting on the swing next to me, staring right at me.

"Why did you leave?" he asks quietly. I know what he's referring to, but I try to delay it as long as I can.

"Does it matter? I left and now I'm back. Let's just leave it at that," I say before digging my feet in the dirt to stop the swing and get up. Not waiting for him to either say something or stop me, I start walking back toward the shop, wanting to get away from Louie and desperately needing to quiet the chaos inside my head. Stopping at this park was a mistake. It made me *feel*. Feel everything, but mostly it made me feel the loss and heartache. And now with him here, trying to dig deep inside my head for answers I don't want to give, I'm desperate to flee. I'm desperate to drown out the voices inside my head and the aching hole inside my chest. I think I have a bottle of something that will do the trick.

I don't make it even five steps before Louie grabs me by my arm and hauls me around to face him. "It just does. Now tell me. Why the fuck did you leave? Why then? Was what we did really that bad? Do you regret it that fucking much?" He's angry now, but not as angry as I am that he won't let it go.

"And if I *do* regret it?" I say through clenched teeth.

I don't regret what happened, at least not in the way he may think. But since he's bringing it up and making me dredge up all these memories— memories of not only the way he made me feel, but what happened after. How after I gave myself to him, I was left with nothing—I want to piss him off and make him think that I do. I want him to hurt like I hurt.

He just stares at me, searching for the truth, but I

won't let him find it. I can't, because if he knows what happened, then it makes it real. And if it's real, then that would mean that it's over. If it's over, then that means I need to forget, and dammit, I can't fucking forget it. It's carved on my skin, it's in my soul. It fucking haunts me while I'm sleeping and even while I'm awake.

Finally, he speaks. "I don't believe that. Not for one fucking second. It may have happened at the wrong time and you may want to regret it, but you don't."

The way that he seems so sure, like there's not a doubt in his mind that I don't feel that way, makes me even angrier. *How fucking dare he!* He doesn't know what I think! He doesn't have the right to stand there and judge me or tell me how I feel.

"You don't know jack fucking shit! I wish that night with you never fucking happened! If it didn't, then he'd still fucking be here! He'd still be a part of my life and the past two years of feeling worthless and like I was to blame wouldn't have fucking happened either. I wouldn't be standing here right now feeling like all the air in my lungs were gone. I wouldn't feel like I died and am now living in a constant state of agony. If I would have never let you fuck me, he'd still be here! But it did fucking happen, and now he's gone."

I swear, if I could shoot fire out of my mouth or lasers out of my eyes, I would have, that's how fucking heated and pissed I am, though I'm taking it out on the wrong person. I know that—God, do I fucking know that, but it doesn't stop me.

"He was always my rock, my every-fucking-thing. He told me that I was better than this and to not throw my life away on any man. Not unless he deserved me. Hendrix always thought I was a good girl, and that no one would ever be worthy of me. But you know what? *I'm* the one who isn't worthy and I *did* give it all away. I threw it all away for you. *You!* And because of that, I'm being punished. Because of that, he's *gone*."

My breathing is rapid and my heart is racing so fast, you probably can't even hear the separate beats anymore. It would sound like one long, loud beat that goes on forever.

I can feel myself getting lightheaded and almost sick to my stomach thinking about what happened, but now I can't stop. I can't stop seeing his face, hearing his voice telling me I fucked up, and the last time I saw him and the vacant look in his eyes. He's gone and I can't fucking stand it, it hurts so bad it burns me from the inside out. Burns me with rage and despair.

In my head, I see his face, and I can hear his laugh. He was so full of life and love for me. But it's all gone. I'll never see his smile or be able to listen to him tell me he loves me. I'll never have the opportunity to hug him or tell him how much I love him or how much he meant to me. He's just *gone*.

I feel tears running down my face and it's all too much. I can't handle this. I just want it all to go away—the anger, the guilt, and the pain.

Suddenly, Louie grabs my shoulders and shakes me—literally shakes me. "Harlow, what the fuck are you talking about?"

There's a hard edge to his voice and I let it fuel

my rage. I let it breath inside of me to allow me to tell him what happened.

"He's dead," I yell. "He's gone and it's all your fault!"

I start to hit his chest with my fists, doing everything in my power to take it out on him. And he lets me.

He's the one who made me feel like I was worthy and that the feelings I felt for him were real. He's the one who I wanted to give myself to and I wanted it. I wanted it! But all it left me with was emptiness. It left me alone.

And I start to break inside. The pieces of concrete around my emotions start to falter that allows the tears to fall.

Louie sees I'm breaking, and just when I think there will be nothing left of me, he wraps his strong arms around me and holds me together. But it's so much more than just holding me together—it's like he's mending what's broken, little by little, just by holding me.

"He's dead," I say on a broken whisper.

Instead of letting me go, shocked and uncertain, he continues to hold me, rubbing my back. "Who, Harlow?" he whispers back.

Without thinking, I just let it all out. "My brother. My *twin* brother. That's why I left. He's dead."

There was a part of me that thought after saying the words out loud, the pain would go away. That it would help me to finally start healing, but it doesn't. It makes me feel *worse*.

Louie pulls back far enough so he can look down

at me, but I can't look at him. It will just add to the whirlwind of feelings that are tearing their way through my body. If I look at him, I'll be pushed over the ledge and I don't think I'll be able to come back from that.

"What happened?" he asks after a silent moment.

His question forces me to finally look into his eyes. I see nothing but concern and pity, which pours more fuel on my anger. I don't need his fucking pity. I don't need *anything* from him!

"You know what? I'm not doing this. Not with you, not with *anyone*," I say, then struggle to release myself from his tight hold, but it's no use. "Let me go!" I yell.

"No. You're going to tell me what happened. You *need* to let it out, Harlow. Keeping it all bottled up inside isn't helping you. It will fester and boil until there's nothing left. Do you understand me? There will be nothing left of you! And I won't fucking let that happen."

"Why the fuck do you care so much about what happens to me? You have it all—you have the friends, the family, and the job. You have everything!" I spit, suddenly not only angry at my brother for what he did, but at Louie, at the world. For everything they could ever dream of having while I'm left with nothing.

Louie shakes me again, this time hard enough that I can feel my teeth clash together. "I care because it's *you*! I care because I can't stand to see you in pain. And I can't go another day without you in my life. Before you left, I *finally* felt like I did have everything. I felt I had that because of *you*. It didn't matter if I had the club or my job, it only mattered that I got to see you every day. That I got to talk to you and make you laugh that beautiful laugh. And it only mattered when I had you in my arms. It killed me when you left. I had no idea where you were or when you'd be back, or if you even *would* come back. I didn't know if it was because of me or if something happened. I died inside the day you left. Can't you see? You matter. You mean more to me than anything has in a very long time."

His words break through the fog of anger and penetrate my shattered heart. They soothe my soul all at the same time. How is that? How can he just look at me and say a few meaningful words and make it seem like my world isn't dark anymore? That my life isn't over?

I hit a breaking point, but it's not the type of breaking point I once feared. This is something I never thought could happen. It feels like an outer shell has been cracked and is finally tumbling down, and what's left inside is able to finally breathe after so long without air. I feel raw, but it feels sort of good. Like, if you've ever broken your arm or your leg and had to wear a cast for weeks, and then when it finally gets taken off your limb can breathe.

After everything that's happened in the past hour, I no longer have any strength left. My legs give out, but I don't fall. Instead, Louie slowly lowers us both to the ground, with me cradled in his lap. He just holds me and rocks me back and forth, whispering over and over again that he's got me and that he's not going anywhere. He has no idea what that last sentence does to me, what it means to me, especially now.

We sit there forever it seems, but when he finally stands with me still cocooned in his arms, I feel like not only is he lifting me, he's lifting this weight that has weighed me down for so long. It makes me feel so free, that my eyelids start to close and sleep starts to take hold of me, but this time, I welcome it.

Before I completely surrender to my sleep-deprived body, I let the words finally leave my mouth. Words that will hopefully free me for good.

"He killed himself."

CHAPTER 7

Louie

Looking down, I see that Harlow is out like a light. I have no doubt that going through everything she did tonight took a lot out of her, but I'd also guess that she hasn't had a decent night's sleep since her brother died. No, since he *killed* himself.

I've never known anyone who has been in a place who has either tried to or has committed suicide. I haven't even known someone who knew someone who had that happen to someone they care about—until Harlow.

I can't imagine what she went through and how she must have felt. And fuck—the past two years having all that hate and anger inside. The only thing I can compare it to is the anger I felt when my dad died. Though, he didn't just die either—he was *taken*. He was murdered in cold blood.

Thinking about it still has that *thing* inside of me roaring and begging to come out. Each of us had someone taken from us, and neither were an accident—though my father didn't choose to leave, where her brother did. That must burn her. She must have asked herself a million times *"Why?"* And from what it sounds like, she didn't have anyone else. Her brother was all she had. So when she found out, she was alone to deal with it. Utterly and completely alone. At least when my father was murdered, I had Mack to keep me together somewhat.

I don't know her whole story. Shit, I didn't even know she had a brother, but from what she said, I think it'd be a pretty fair statement that she doesn't have any other family.

It cuts me deep that she never considered me, Dani, and my brothers her family, though. Since the day she started working at the shop, she became a part of us, just like Dani said. And even if she didn't believe that then, what about when she and I got closer? Why didn't she come to *me*, at least? *You know why, dipshit. She thought her brother dying was punishment for her fucking you.*

There's no point trying to figure out what she was thinking or wonder why she felt she couldn't come back right now. She's sleeping. She needs her rest, and then tomorrow I can get the answer I need. Maybe she'll get the answers she needs too.

Not wanting to wake her up, I decide that I'll just carry her back to the shop. She's been staying in the upstairs apartment, and I'm sure Dani is still at the shop. She'll have a spare key and can let us in. Then, I can lay her down and keep watch over her.

If she thinks for one minute I'm leaving her side and letting her go through this alone, she's wrong.

One thing I remember more than anything else is when my dad died, Mack was always there for me. Even when I didn't want him to be. He may not have hovered, but he made sure that I knew he was there for anything I needed—even giving me the choice and opportunity to kill the bastard responsible for my dad's death.

It takes me a little longer to walk back to the shop, but I wanted to walk at a slower pace as to not jostle Harlow around and wake her up.

When I walk in front of the door, I look in and see Dani already rushing toward us.

Before she opens the door, she must realize that Harlow isn't hurt, but sleeping because she slows her pace marginally and removes the bell from above the door before opening it so the noise doesn't wake her.

"What happened? Is she all right?" Dani whispers, but I can hear the worry in her voice. And I know Dani, when she's worried, she better have an answer quick, because regardless if Harlow is sleeping, she'll wake her ass up, poking and prodding her to make sure she's all right.

"She's fine, just sleeping. Can you get the door to her apartment so I can lay her down?" I whisper back quickly. I know after I lay Harlow down, Dani will be relentless until I tell her what happened. You learn pretty fast that when it comes to Dani, you don't really have a choice in matters. What she wants, she'd better get or there will be hell to pay.

Dani nods and I follow her inside as she grabs the spare key. Then, I follow her out the back door and up the steps. She quietly opens the door but before going up, she turns to look over her shoulder. "Don't think that you're getting out of explaining. I expect answers as soon as you put our girl in bed." She doesn't wait for a reply because she doesn't need one. Like I said, you better give her what she wants.

While I head into the bedroom to lay Harlow down, Dani waits in the living room. I'm glad for that because if she saw me taking my sweet ass time making sure Harlow was lying in a comfortable position, made sure she was covered up, and then just stared at her sleeping peacefully for a minute, she would have slapped me upside the head and probably pulled me out of the room by my ear. Okay, that may be over exaggerating a little, but maybe not. This *is* Dani we're talking about.

By the time I turn the light off and close the door behind me, Dani is already pacing and biting her fingernails. That's a new habit she picked up after the kids were born, though I can't say I blame her. If I had kids, I'd probably have to do something extreme to get my frustrations and nervousness out too. Nail biting is a safe way to do that I guess.

When she finally notices me, she storms over. "What happened?"

I don't want to give too much away, knowing Harlow wouldn't want that. If she wants Dani to know the specifics, she'll tell her in her own time.

"I can't tell you everything, but she finally got some things out about what happened while she was away. I think she's going to be fine now, but we need to be there for her. She's gonna need us now more than ever." I pray that she doesn't push me because it will just turn into a fight and Harlow needs her rest, not be woken up by Dani and I arguing.

Dani's quiet for a moment. I know it's not what she wants—she wants to know specifically what happened, in detail—but I'm hoping she'll take it for what it's worth. Harlow opened up and that was the first step. Now, all we can do is be there for her if she needs us and let her set the pace.

I can see tears gather in Dani's eyes. She's still fucking badass for a chick, but now she's okay with showing her emotions. She no longer holds everything inside or puts on a show as if nothing fazes her. I'm actually relieved to see her this way.

"I just want our girl back—for *good*. If that means I have to wait until she comes to me with this whenever she's ready, then I'm okay with that. I'm just glad she told someone because I could tell something happened, and it was eating away at her."

I know what she means, but I think after tonight things will be better. Harlow still has a long way to go, but this is a new beginning, maybe for both of us. God knows I couldn't handle it if she walked away from me again. I don't know if I love her, but I know I care a lot for her and I want her to be happy. And that I need her in my life.

"That's all we can do. We just have to be there for her and show her we aren't going away, no matter what happens. She may lash out and tell us she doesn't need us, but she does. And when she's ready, she'll talk to you, I know she will." I pull Dani in for a hug because I know this must be tearing her up inside. When Harlow and Sara came into her life, she finally found a connection I think she desperately needed. Sure, she has the boys and was happy, but there's something about having another female companion that is so much better. But what the fuck do I know, I'm a dude, but that's the way it seems to me.

"Why don't you head on home to your man and your little ones? Lord knows I'm sure Blaze is chomping at the bit because you aren't home yet," I say with a laugh. Blaze has loosened up quite a bit and even though they don't fight as much anymore, he's still very protective and domineering when it comes to Dani.

She laughs and wipes a single tear that escaped her eye. "Yeah, I bet he is, but I'm sure a little strip tease will have him forget his worry real quick," she says with a wink.

Shaking my head, I gently push her toward the door. "I did *not* need to know that. Get outta here before I call Blaze and have him come carry your ass outta here caveman style."

Laughing, she moves her eyebrows up and down. "Don't tease me with a good time. You know I love it when my man goes caveman on me."

"Get the fuck out, woman. You're too much."

When she reaches the door, she turns around to face me and all the humor has left her face. "I know sometimes you don't think it, but you are a good man, Louie. Harlow will come around, and when she does, she'll know it again too. You're good for each other, so don't push her away, yeah?"

Her words give me pause because there are so

many times that I don't feel like a good man—I feel like Lucifer himself. I know I tend to push people away when things get rough, but I'm hoping that this time I can change that. Maybe since I now know what it's like not to have Harlow in my life, it will help stop me from pushing her away.

Nodding, I give her a small smile to let her know I hear her and will do my best.

"Night, Louie," Dani says, and then she shuts the door quietly behind her.

Letting out a long breath, trying to release the stress of the day, I walk back toward the bedroom. Harlow is still sound asleep and doesn't seem to have moved even an inch.

Stripping off my shirt and boots, I gently climb into bed beside her. I'm not one hundred percent sure this is a good idea, but I can't seem to care. I need to feel her next to me, know that she's really here, and that she's not going away.

In her sleep, she rolls over and snuggles up right next to me. Fuck, I've missed her. Not only like this, but everything about the way we used to be. She came into my life when things were difficult with Dani, and even though we got past it and I could never replace the friendship we have, Harlow was like a soothing balm on my soul. She became my best friend.

Closing my eyes, I fall into a deep sleep with a smile on my face. Things are going to be okay. I'll make sure of it.

***

I don't know what time it is, but it feels like I just closed my eyes when I feel Harlow sit up suddenly before she starts sobbing so loud I can literally feel my heart break with every sound of pain that escapes her lips. Sitting up with her, I pull her into my arms and start to rock her.

"Shh, it's okay, baby, I'm here. I've got you," I say in a soothing tone.

We sit like that for a while—me rocking her and whispering words of assurance and her crying—until she finally settles down enough to speak.

"I-I'm sorry. I didn't m-mean to wake you," she stutters around a few errant tears.

"You have nothing to be sorry for," I tell her. I know she still has a long, hard road ahead of her, and she doesn't need to add to that. Plus, I'm glad I was here for her when she needed me. It makes me wonder how many nights she's awoken like this and no one was there to hold her and tell her it would be all right. At least, I don't think anyone was with her. Thinking of her in the arms of another man has my jaw clenching and a red haze drifting into my sight, but I tamp that shit down. She doesn't need me questioning her right now or going on a rampage of misplaced jealousy.

"Do you want to talk about it?" I ask after I've calmed myself down.

She's quiet for so long, I wonder if she's fallen asleep in my arms. But then I hear her take a long breath and let it out before speaking.

"Our parents died before we were even old enough to really remember them. I have no memories of them, and as far as I know, neither did

Hendrix. We didn't have any other family, so we were placed into foster care right after the car accident that took their lives. I'm not sure how long it took us to be placed in an actual house with an actual family because I don't remember the beginning, but my first memory of being with a family was a pleasant one. The husband and wife were amazing and treated us real good. But we weren't there long. They had their own baby and suddenly we weren't there anymore. I guess I can't blame them for wanting us out when they finally had an actual blood child to care for."

Harlow releases me, and figuring she needs some space to talk about what she's sharing I let her go, even though it is physically painful for me to do so, and watch as she stares off into space.

"After that, the places we were at sort of blended together. A mixture of group homes and shitty foster parents. They weren't all horrible, they just weren't as nice and caring as our first. They wouldn't buy us new clothes, always giving us crappy hand-me-downs that barely fit. And the only good meal we had was when we were in school. Sure, they gave us food, but we had to cook it ourselves and it was always something like cold sandwiches or mac and cheese. I never had a problem with those meals before, but when you have them every day, let's just say that if I never ate that shit again it'd be too soon."

Now, she's up and pacing around the room, fidgeting with her shirt. I know the feeling of not being able to stand still because your skin crawls with the memories of the past, so I understand what she's doing, but I need her to continue—I need her to let me in. I want to be there for her, but I can't do that if I don't know what happened. Yeah, I know her brother killed himself, but I have no idea what led up to it, or if *she* even knows. But the background she's giving me could help me help her figure it out too. I hope anyway.

"Then, when we were sixteen, we were put into a house with a man that already had one foster kid living with him. He didn't have a wife, but our case worker said that he was a great father figure and was happy to take us in, even though we were older than the kids he usually fostered. That right there should have put up red flags, but at that point, it was just another place for us to lay our heads at night. We were just counting down the days till we would be kicked out of the system and have to be on our own. As much as we looked forward to it, we dreaded it all the same. I mean, how would we survive on our own? We knew we would never be able to make it into a college, and even if we did, we had no money to pay for it. What else did that leave us? Working a shitty job with a shitty wage to pay for a shitty apartment? But we'd do what we'd have to do. We'd stick together and we'd take it one day at a time. That's all we could do."

"We were there about six months before I noticed what was going on, or at least, what I *thought* was going on. The other kid in the house with us was a girl. She was about twelve years of age. She was quiet and seemed off, but I just figured it was because she had a shitty upbringing before she got there. I never thought that what she was *actually* scared of was being in *that* house until one night I heard her crying. I could barely hear it, thought maybe I was imagining it, but when I got up to check, I realized what I heard was real and saw the cause of the outcry for myself. The foster dad was touching her—sexually. He wasn't having sex with her, but he might as well have been. I was so scared; I didn't know what to do. I mean, it's not like I could have stopped him, ya know? But I had to do *something*, so I backed away and made as much noise as I could going to the bathroom almost right across from her room. I didn't go to the bathroom though. I stood quietly with my ear to the door to see if he left her alone. He did, but he told her to keep her mouth shut or he would shut it for her—*permanently*."

"When I thought I had spent enough time in there, I quietly walked out of the bathroom and when I passed her door, she was alone but still crying. I should have gone to her, asked if she was all right, but considering the warning she got, would she really tell me? Did I even want to know? So what did I do? I just gave her a sad smile and walked back to my room."

I can tell she regrets not doing anything and how she acted upsets her, but she's right; what could she have done? She would have risked herself *and* that little girl by doing something. She did the only thing she could do to stop him and it worked. She got him away from the girl, if only for a little while. That has to count for something. But the look on Harlow's face tells me she thinks she should have done more. I want to tell her she did the right thing and there was nothing else she could have done, but before I can open my mouth, she continues with her story.

"The next day, I pulled Hendrix aside and told him we needed to leave. He had changed as well in the last few months since being there—he lost weight and looked like he hadn't slept in weeks. I thought maybe he saw what I saw or maybe knew something more, but I couldn't bring myself to ask. After witnessing what I did the night before, I didn't want to talk about it or hear something worse, so I was sure Hendrix didn't want to talk about it either. He just nodded and said I was right and he'd figure something out for us to get out of there and soon. It was a week later that he came to my room in the middle of the night and said it was time to leave. I didn't question him and I didn't ask if we should bring the girl along with us. How would we support ourselves, let alone another kid? So we just left her there, left her alone in that house with that monster to fend for herself."

I have no idea what to say to that. To be honest, I probably would have done the same thing. When you're that young, you shouldn't even have to worry about taking care of yourself, let alone another child. Shit, you're a child yourself!

"Hendrix dropped out of school and got three different jobs. We found a one-bedroom apartment an hour away from where the foster home was and that's where we stayed until I graduated high school. He said that I needed to stay in school—I argued that I could get a job too, help with the bills, but he wouldn't have it. Said I needed an education so I could better my life. So I didn't question him; I just did what he said. I let him work himself to the bone. I knew it was hard on him and I told him every day that I loved him and that when I graduated, I'd get a good job and it would be *my* turn to take care of *him*. He just smiled and said, 'I know, Princess.' But that day never came, and it never will now. When I graduated, he told me to go off and find a job I loved. Once I had a place set up for myself, he'd follow. I begged him to come with me, but he said he had things to finish there, but as soon as things on my end were solid, he'd find me."

By now, she's stopped and just stares out the window. I want to go to her, but I worry it will be too much for her. After everything she went through, would I push her too far by taking her in my arms? *Fuck it.* I need to hold her and she needs it too. If she breaks, I'll hold her together. I'll be her rock, the person to lift her back up.

Getting up quietly, I walk across the room and wrap my arms around her from behind. "Then what happened?" I ask after I feel her relax into my embrace.

"I got too busy in my own life. I moved around a lot, looking for the right place to call home. I didn't forget about him, I swear I didn't. I called him at least once a week and told him that I was close to finding a place and a good job. He would just tell me that he was fine and that he had almost everything in place there as well. I don't know what things he had to take care of, and I never asked, but I figured it was just tying up loose ends at his jobs and getting rid of that apartment."

"Then, when I came here, I knew I'd found the place, but I wanted to wait till I had enough money to get out of the crappy apartment I was in and get something bigger for me and him to share. I was almost there too, so I didn't call him for a few weeks, thinking I'd call him when I had everything in place and could tell him the good news. But before I could, I got the phone call from the hospital, telling me that my brother was dead. I didn't believe them at first, but then it sank in. Hendrix was dead and it was all my fault. I should have pushed more for him to come with me right away. I should have done more to find a job and place sooner; I should have worked harder. I should have—" She lets loose a sob.

"And now he's g-gone. How could he leave me here all alone? How could he think that I'd be okay without him? Why? Why did he leave?" She's full on crying now but there's no anger in her outburst. It's all sadness, pain, and regret.

Taking her in my arms, I walk us over to the bed and lay her down beside me, making sure I never let her go in the process. "It's going to be okay. I know it doesn't seem that way, but I promise, it will get better. I'm here, we're *all* here for you, Harlow. Let us help you carry this burden. Let us be there for you," I whisper into her hair, but I know she hears me when I feel her nod. I feel her finally lose the fight to herself and accept that she doesn't have to be alone, that we are here for her.

Minutes later, I feel her breathing even out and her tears dry up. Knowing that she trusts me enough to tell me everything that happened and that I'm allowed to comfort her warms me from the inside out. My heart swells and I finally realize I *do* love this girl. I'm still not sure if it's the kind of love that means she's my soulmate or anything like that. But I do know I love her in the way that I don't want to be without her, I want to be there for her, and be her friend, her *best* friend. And I'm going to do everything in my power to make sure she knows what she means to me. I'll make her believe that she has me and the club, that we aren't leaving her, and that we'll always be there for her, no matter what.

CHAPTER 8

Harlow

I'm having the same dream I've had every night I can remember since I found out that Hendrix was gone.

It starts with us as children—being happy and carefree—then it jumps to the night we left our last foster home. I was so scared, but Hendrix was there to tell me it was all going to be okay. Then it jumps again to the day I left after graduating, but instead of him pushing me to leave, he's begging to go with me. I just ignore him and pack up my things and walk out the door, all the while he's crying and yelling that he needs me and that I can't leave him there. But this time, instead of me getting into my shitty car and driving off like I do every other night in my dream, I stop and turn toward him. I expect to see his tear-stained face, but instead, I see him smile at me.

"It took you long enough," he says as he takes

the few steps toward me so we are standing face-to-face, close enough that I could touch him but I don't. I'm afraid that if I do or if I say anything, this dream with turn back into my nightmare.

"It's okay, Harlow. I'm not going anywhere." He reaches out and touches my face tenderly like he used to.

"But you did. You left me," I say quietly, still afraid this will all go away—that he'll leave me again.

"I know, but I'll always be with you. Right here," he says and places his hand over my heart. "And right here." The hand that was on my heart moves to gently brush against my temple.

"It's not the same."

"I know." I need more. I need to know why.

"Why did you do it, Hendrix? Why did you leave me? Didn't you know I needed you? That I can't be happy in my life without you? You're my twin, Hendrix. My other half. I need you," I say, feeling a single tear falling down my face, but Hendrix catches it before it falls to the ground.

"I know you won't understand, but I had to go. I was never meant to stay; I see that now. My job was to make sure you were strong enough to be on your own, and I did that. My time was over, but yours is still here. You need to stop living in the past and stop blaming yourself and live. You have people in your life—family—that need you. It's time to let me go."

He takes a step back, and I panic. "No. Please don't leave me. Not yet. I have so many questions, please. I love you, please don't leave. I need you,

Hendrix!" I yell, trying to walk toward him, but I can't move.

"You're wrong, Princess. You don't need me, and that's okay. I'll always be with you, but I need to go now. Read the letter I wrote you, it will tell you all you need to know. I love you, sis. Always and forever."

Then he's gone. I want to cry, but I can't, my body won't let me, so I just stand there and stare at the place where he stood only moments ago. I hate that I feel this calming peace come over my body, but I know that it's right. What he said was right. I don't believe some of the things he said, but I know that I need to move on. I'll always remember him, but I need to live my life and let him live through me. That's how I can remember him and honor his memory. As much as I don't want to, I need to let him go.

I open my eyes, and the sunlight is shining in through the windows. The sun's rays are shining directly onto a sleeping Louie and I know it's my brother's way of telling me that he is my future. It's him showing me that it's okay to love and move on, and that I should be with Louie. I can feel it in my heart that my brother would approve of him.

Raising my hand, I touch his face gently. I have missed him so much and I realize now that staying away for so long was wrong on so many levels. Not only did I hurt myself, but I hurt him and everyone else here by doing so. That's something I'm going to have to apologize for, but first, I need to *feel* Louie—all of him.

Trailing my hand down his face to his stomach, I hear his sharp intake of breath when I touch below his belly button. Not low enough to hit pay dirt, but enough that he knows where this is leading. My heart rate picks up in anticipation and my hand starts to shake with nerves. I haven't done this since the first and last time that Louie and I had sex—my *first* and *only* time—but I need this. I *want* this.

"What are you doing?" he says, voice raspy from sleep.

"Tell me to stop if you don't want this, but I need you, Louie. I need to feel you inside me. I need you to make me feel alive again, like I know only you can do," I say before finally moving my hand down further, touching his hard cock straining against his jeans.

"Fuck, I need to you too, Low, but are you sure? We can wait. After last night—" he starts to say, but I cut him off by grabbing him firmly in my hand.

"I'm done talking, so if you don't want this, you better stop me now." I don't waste any time grabbing the button on his jeans and lowering his zipper, but he catches my hand before I can get any further.

Nerves jump out at me again and I worry that he's actually going to tell me no, to stop, but my fears are quickly dashed aside when he pushes me onto my back and takes my lips in a rough kiss.

"Fuck, I've missed you," he says between kisses. Not giving me any time to reply, he leans back in to drink from my lips. And I mean that almost literally. It's like he's trying to devour me, starting with my mouth, but you won't hear me complaining. I've missed him so much these last couple years; I can't believe I even made it an hour without him to at least *talk* to, let alone have him kissing me, touching me, *loving* me. The night we shared before I left town was one of the happiest days of my life, but being in his arms now and with his lips on mine, I know that it will soon be overshadowed by better days and memories.

With my head back in the game, and my body screaming at me to move faster to get him naked and inside of me, I reach down to unbutton his jeans, but am pleasantly surprised when I notice they are already unbuttoned. That's good, because I really didn't want to waste time fumbling with his button in my haste to get them off of him.

Going right for his zipper, I start to lower it when Louie lifts his head slightly and stops my movements with his concerned gaze.

"Are you sure about this, Low? I mean, I can wait—fuck, it might *kill* me—but we don't have to do this today. You've been through hell, I'm sure I don't even know the half of it, but last night had to have taken a lot out of you too. So if this isn't something you want right now, I'm okay with it."

My heart almost breaks with the compassion and love I hear in his voice. I know he means well, and a part of me loves him even more for thinking of my feelings and what I've been through at a time like this, but the rest of me just wants him to fuck me already.

"Louie, I don't know how to put this lightly, so I'm just going to come out and say it. I want this. I want *you*. So will you shut up already and just fuck me?"

Looking deep into my eyes for only a second, but long enough to know that what I said is the truth—that I want this, *need* this—then he's on me. It's a full attack to my body and senses. His mouth is on mine as he rips the shirt from my body. Before I know it, I'm completely naked and I feel his hard cock enter me in one powerful thrust. It's so filling in more ways than one. He not only entered my pussy, he entered my heart, my soul.

"Fuck," he grunts. "So fucking tight."

And he doesn't stop. He's a man possessed and nothing will stand in the way of his need for me and I feel the same way. I'm desperate to feel all of him and want nothing more than to stay like this, wrapped around his body with him inside of me forever.

I start to feel that amazing build that starts deep in my stomach and travels all the way to the tips of my toes and down my fingers. I swear I can even feel it building through the strands of my hair. It's intense. More than I remember our first time being.

"Louie," I beg him, but unsure what it is I need. What he makes my body do and how he makes me feel is almost too much for me to bear. I don't know if I should tell him to stop and give my body a break or to keep going. All I know is that my body is tingling all over and I feel drunk. My mind is getting hazy and I feel like I'm floating.

"Who's body is this?" He growls the question, but it isn't harsh.

"It's yours. Take it," I yell, scratching his back, begging him to do as I say. I want him to take me in every way possible.

"Fucking right it is," he says, punctuating it with a hard thrust that has me seeing stars. "And I plan on taking it. Over, and over, and over."

He thrusts faster and I know it won't be long before I fall over the cliff into ecstasy.

"Come for me, Harlow. Give me what you kept from me for so long. Give me what's *mine*."

Like a slave to him, I obey. The sound of his voice and the meaning of his words do me in and I come harder than I ever thought a woman could come. It feels like my whole body is being ripped in half but I don't want it to end. It's the most pleasant pain I've ever felt.

Screaming out his name with my release, I hear him grunt and follow me into bliss. And suddenly I know without a doubt I will never be able to live my life without him. He is it for me. If he was no longer a part of this world, I would cease to exist as well. It's like that saying in one of my favorite movies, *Backdraft*—"You go, we go." If he dies, I die with him. It may not be the same moment or same way, but I know that I would soon follow. And written on my death certificate, the cause of death will state a broken heart.

After he comes, he drops his weight on me completely, but it feels good to be smothered by him. It makes me feel like no matter what, he won't ever let me go.

When he finally moves off of me, he rolls onto his side and pulls me right up against him so my back is to his front. I hope he does this for the rest of my life, because it makes me feel cherished. I love the way he wraps his arms around me and even though we're just lying here, he squeezes me like he's afraid if he doesn't hold on tight, I'll disappear. I guess I'm to blame for that fear, but I'll do whatever it takes to make sure he knows I'm here to stay, that I'm his.

I don't know how long we lay there, just basking in each other's company, but when I finally speak, my voice is hoarse from being silent for so long. And I'm sure all my moaning and screaming out Louie's name probably didn't help either.

"I have something I need to do." After my dream, I know what I have to do, but I want Louie with me. I need him to help me through this. I know it's going to be very hard for me to do. I can't do it alone.

"Okay. Do you want me to go with you?" he asks, seemingly reading my mind.

"Yes." I untangle myself from his arms and get out of bed. Grabbing a pair of sleep shorts and a tank top, I look back to where he still lays.

"Are you coming?"

"I just did, and I plan to come again and again and again..." he says with a sexy smirk, letting the sentence drop off.

His comment makes me giggle, and it feels good knowing I can smile and be happy even though what I'm about to do is going to be hard.

"Ha ha. You're hilarious." Rolling my eyes, I try to keep my smile hidden but it's no use. This man makes me smile when I thought there was nothing left in this world that could make me happy. I walk toward the door and say over my shoulder, "Now get the fuck up and meet me in the living room." There's no malice in my voice so he knows I'm not mad, but I said it with enough urgency that he knows to get a move on.

I head right toward the kitchen, knowing I'll need something to calm me, so I grab a coffee mug down and fill it with water before putting it in the microwave. I think this is a situation that calls for tea, not coffee. I'll be jumpy enough, no need to add loads of caffeine on top of it.

Louie comes strutting out of the room as I'm adding sugar to my tea. When he reaches me, he leans down and kisses my head before grabbing a bottle of water out of the fridge. "So where are we going?"

I take a small sip of my tea, then look at him. "Nowhere." I love messing with him and only giving him one word answers. I know it pisses him off because he has to be in the know about everything. We used to play around like this all the time and it feels nice to get back into our old routines of goading each other.

"Now who's the funny one? But seriously, where are we going?"

"I *am* being serious. We aren't going anywhere."

"Okay, well if we don't have any place to be, what was is it that you have to do that couldn't wait?"

Wanting to stall, even a little bit, I take my tea and head into the living room, but don't sit down. Instead, I turn to look at Louie and motion him over to the couch. Without further prompting, he sits down and waits. I guess it's now or never.

"Before my brother killed himself, he wrote me a letter. When I arrived at the hospital, the police officer who was handling the case said that they found it on him. It was addressed to me. I never read it."

He quietly contemplates what I just shared, then speaks. "So I'm guessing you want to read the letter now." It's not a question, but I nod to answer anyway.

"Why now? Why today? What changed your mind?"

I think about my answer before I speak. I don't want him to think I'm crazy when I tell him about my dream, but that *is* the reason, so I guess he deserves to know.

"I had a dream last night," I say, then walk over to a box that I never unpacked. No matter where I went or how long I stayed here, I never have unpacked it. It's full of things I couldn't leave behind that belonged to my brother. I don't even remember what's all in there. After I packed it that day, I just put the box in my front seat whenever I was on the road, and kept the box close by wherever I was staying. It was like that box signified my brother and he was always with me.

But it's time I finally open it. Maybe put some of the things around my apartment so there's a part of Hendrix here, and whenever I walk through the door, I'll be able to see them. But first, I need to open the letter he wrote me. His *goodbye* letter.

Opening the box, the letter sits on top of everything. Grabbing it without looking at anything else, I walk back over to the couch and sit down beside Louie.

"I had a dream last night. At first, I thought it was just like the one I have every night where Hendrix begs me not to leave him and I do it anyway. He cries and begs me not to go, to take him with, but I don't even turn around to face him. I just leave. But something was different this time. Instead of me leaving him behind, I turned around to *finally* face him." I pause for a minute, trying to gather myself before continuing.

"It was so *real*, Louie. It was like he was really there in my dream, the real him, not just some figment of my imagination, ya know? He came to me last night and spoke to me. He said he was okay and that I had to let him go. That it was time to move on."

It still pains me a little to think about letting him go, but I know now that it is what has to be done. And just because I finally accept his fate, that's he's really gone for good, that doesn't mean that I'll forget him. If anything, this will allow me to stop all my negative thoughts where he's concerned and let the light and good memories back through again. And fuck, have I missed those memories of my brother.

"He told me that I needed to read his letter. He knew I hadn't read it, Louie, that's how I know this was real, that it was him. I haven't been able to bring myself to read that letter, afraid about what it would say and angry that he wrote me a letter instead of telling me in person. But it's finally time to put those fears and angry thoughts behind me. To put this whole thing behind me. I *need* to read his letter, but I can't do it by myself."

Without me even asking him, he takes me in his arms and lets me know that he's here for me. We stay like this, locked in this soothing embrace, for what feels like hours, but I'm in no rush to move. Maybe we can stay just like this while I read my brother's note.

Thinking about it now, and having it in my hand, I become afraid again. There's no anger this time, just pure fear of what's inside. Is it something I really want to know?

Louie must feel me tense, because he pulls away just enough to look in my eyes. "Hey, it's okay. I'll be right here beside you. I'm not going anywhere. You can read his letter and then I can help you start healing."

"I-I'm scared," I whisper, feeling tears start to fall. What if I'm not strong enough to read his words?

"I know you're scared, but you have to do this. He wanted you to know something or else he wouldn't have written this for you. He knew you could handle it, and I do too."

"Will you read it to me?" I ask Louie, praying he agrees. I'm not sure I'm strong enough to read it myself, something that my brother must have written in pain and torment.

"Are you sure?"

Knowing if I speak now, my voice will break and I'll crumble before I even hear my brother's words, I just nod, then hand the letter over to Louie with shaky hands. Taking it from me, he looks at me once more before he opens the envelope to pull out the letter with what I hope are answers that have been untold for too long.

CHAPTER 9

Louie

I don't really want to do this. I have a bad feeling that whatever is inside this letter is going to set her back from what little progress she seemed to have made overnight. I said that she can handle it, but a part of me wonders if she can. Even with my help, will she be able to heal after hearing her brother's final words?

I know she thinks this letter from her brother holds all the answers, but what if it doesn't? What if what was so hard for him to bear that he took his own life will haunt Harlow for the rest of hers? Or worse yet, what if she can't live with herself after hearing it?

"Louie. I'll be fine. I just can't read it myself. And I know whatever it is that he wrote will be hard, but I realize now that I have people in my life to help me through it. I don't want to be alone anymore, and I'm not. I have Dani. I have *you*," she says with conviction. I just hope that after all is said and done, she still feels that way.

Opening the envelope, I pull the letter out. Unfolding it slowly, I take a deep breath. If this is what she wants, I will do it—for her.

Scanning the letter, I look up into her sad eyes. But it's not just sadness I see in their depths; there's determination and hope there too.

Looking down at the letter again, I read it out loud to her.

Harlow,

I'm sorry. I wish I could say that I regret my actions and that if I could go back and do it all again, that I wouldn't have done what I did. But I can't because this is exactly what was supposed to happen. You may not see it now, or even want to believe it ever, but it's the truth. My only hope is that you will know that I love you more than anything and hope that one day you can forgive me.

Before you read any further, I need you to understand something. Our life wasn't the best, but I did my best to shelter you from all the bad things in the world. I may not have been able to completely keep it away from you, but I hope when you look back on our time as children, *you will have happy memories, and not memories tainted with pain and sadness.*

I've been going over what I wanted to write to you for weeks now; unsure how much I should tell you. But in the end, you deserve to know the truth. I just hope that it leaves you with peace and not sadness or anger.

Please know that what happened was not your fault. Don't blame yourself for things you didn't know or things that were beyond your control. So if you take anything away from this letter, take with you the fact that I love you and did everything I could to show you that love.

I stop reading to check on Harlow—gauge how she is handling what has been said so far. She's sitting on the couch with her hands clasped tightly together in her lap. She's staring hard at her hands like *they* hold all the answers, not the letter I'm holding.

I wish she'd look at me so I can read her eyes, but it's probably for the best. I need to read this letter for her and if I see the pain inside her eyes, I may not be able to continue reading.

Breathing deep, I continue.

Do you remember our last foster home?

I'm sure you do, but for different reasons than me. Growing up in the system as we did, we knew too well that some places were better than others. But the last one was the final straw. I regret not getting us out of there sooner, but there were things that prevented me from being able to leave.

We had a foster sister. Rayanne. She was so innocent and sweet. Too good for this world. You don't know much about her because she was quiet and tried to blend into the shadows, but you would have loved her. I did.

Rayanne was an orphan because her mother was killed by her father right after she was born, then her father took his own life. It was never known why her dad did what he did, but she seemed at peace with it. She always tried to find the good in people, always looked for the silver lining. Her heart was pure and couldn't stand to see the bad in people, even when they hurt her.

I regret to say I'm one of those people that hurt her. Now I know what you're probably thinking; I would never hurt someone, especially if they are family. But you see, there are times when you have no choice. There are times where it's the better option. If you were forced to make a decision, what would you choose? Hurt someone as young and innocent as Rayanne or watch them be tortured far worse than you could inflict? It's a choice I hope you never have to make, but I chose the first option. I thought that if I were the one hurting her, that it wouldn't be as bad as what could have happened to her. And I was right, but only to a certain extent.

I was young and naïve, stupid really. I thought if I did what I was told, that nothing else would happen. I kept these secrets from you to protect you and prayed that what was happening would never touch you. And I think I succeeded. But secrets were kept from me too. While I was protecting you and doing my best to help her, she was protecting me. Keeping quiet what was going on when I wasn't around.

The night I came to you and told you

we were leaving was the night I found out what she was keeping secret. I wanted to save her too, but it was already too late.

I went to her room to tell her the plan. We were all leaving, getting out of that place for good. But when I opened her door, I found her lying in bed...covered in blood. And beside her, a note telling me she was sorry. That she couldn't do it anymore. And then she told me what she had been keeping from me. Now I'm going to tell you what I've been keeping from you.

I know what he's going to say before I read the next line. I could tell where this tragic story was leading the whole time I was reading this to Harlow. And going by the tears streaming down her face, she knows too.

"We don't have to read the rest, babe," I say just loud enough for her to hear me, but my voice cracks. Of all the things I thought this letter would say, I never guessed this. Drugs, gambling, depression—anything but this.

"No. I have to know for sure, Louie."

I wait till her eyes are on mine before saying, "I'll finish the letter. But promise me, Harlow. Promise that after, we will talk about this. That you won't hold it all inside and let it eat away at you."

Harlow nods, but I need her to say it. "*Promise* me."

She takes a deep breath, then whispers, "I promise, Louie. As long as you help me through it, I won't withdraw into myself. I *promise*."

Reaching out my hand, I wait till she places hers into mine, then pull her on my lap. I need her close. I need to feel her, to know she's here and that I can hold her—*comfort* her—when she needs it.

A few weeks after we moved in, the foster dad came into my room late one night. I was so scared. He told me to keep my mouth shut and to follow him out to the garage. He said if I made one noise, he would take you instead. I didn't know what he was going to do or who was involved, but I knew I couldn't let him take you. So I went. I followed him down the stairs, out the back door, and into the garage.

Once inside, he went to the middle of the room where there was a latch on the ground—a door. I didn't ask any questions. I crawled down a cold, metal ladder that led to a dark underground room.

The space was small, with only one

lightbulb to offer a way to see. But I wish it had been pitch black so I wouldn't have had to see what I saw. It haunts me to this day.

Rayanne was down there, chained to the wall, naked. She was shivering, her face was wet with tears, but she didn't make a noise.

I was told to take my clothes off and have sex with her. He said that if I didn't do it, someone else would. So I did it. I did everything he told me to do while he videotaped it.

This happened every night. Over and over again. I could do nothing to stop it. The only thing that kept me somewhat sane was that I thought I was saving you...saving her. I thought if I was the one doing this to her, then he wouldn't find someone else to do it. Someone older, meaner. But I was wrong.

What I didn't know was that before he would come to get me, he would force himself on Rayanne. Do things to her that I can't even fathom.

She couldn't do it anymore, so she took

her own life. She told me that I needed to take you away from there so what happened to her wouldn't happen to you. She said that you needed me more than she did. So I took you and we ran, but I could never run away from what I did. And when Rayanne came to me in a dream, she told me she didn't blame me for what happened. That she loved me and she was in a better place.

I wanted that too, Harlow. The only purpose I had in life was to make sure you were okay, and I'm fine with that. So I made sure that you were happy and doing good, then I decided it was time for me to join Rayanne.

I know you must hate me for what I kept from you and for leaving you, but please understand that it's better this way. I had my life and did what I set out to do, which was protect you as best I could. Now you need to move on with the life you've made and be happy. Let me go and know I'm happy. Know that I love you and will always watch over you. You'll always be my Princess, but I need

to be with my Angel now.
Please forgive me, Harlow.
Love you always and forever,
Hendrix

By the end of the letter, Harlow is shaking and crying to the point she can barely breathe. "Shh...it's okay, I've got you." I try my best to comfort her, but *fuck*! How do you comfort someone after they learn that the person they love, their sibling, was sexually abused as a child and killed themselves because of it? And to also learn that another innocent child was involved as well, and that child *also* killed themselves.

Instead of talking, I just rock Harlow back and forth on the couch and hold her tight. I need her to know I'm here for her. We can talk later, but right now, she just needs the silence to digest what she learned and to come to terms with what happened.

***

An hour later, she's finally calmed down enough to speak.

"Why haven't you left yet?" Her voice is hoarse from crying.

"What? Why would I leave?" I ask, confused and a little pissed off that she thinks so little of me to think that I would.

"I don't know. I mean, this can't be how you thought you'd spend your day. I'm sure you have better things to do then to watch me break apart and try to put the pieces back together again."

I lean back a little so I can look into her eyes. "I'm not going anywhere, Harlow. I *want* to be here for you. When are you going to get it through that thick head of yours that I care about you and want to help you? You're stuck with me, babe. I'm not leaving you. Not now...not ever." I know those are strong words and she may not believe them, but I don't think I've ever spoken truer words in my life. I will never leave her. Even if she decides to run again, I will find her.

She may have found out why her brother killed himself and what he went through to protect her, but I found something out too. I need her in my life. I'm not sure I could live without her again.

"Come on. Let's get out of here," I say, jumping up with her still in my arms. "Let's do something crazy."

Wiping the tears from her face, she looks at me with the most life I've seen in her eyes since she's gotten back. Shit, maybe even ever.

Smiling, she says, "Hell yes. Let's go *live*."

CHAPTER 10

Harlow

It's been two weeks since Louie read me the letter my brother left me before he killed himself. I still feel some anger toward him, and certainly sadness and pain for what he went through, but I have a better understanding of why he made the choices he made. I wish I could go back in time and change what happened, but that's not how it works. Life isn't a Nintendo game where you get a do-over.

After Louie read the letter, and I cried until I had no more tears, we went to the park. It was a place I could feel connected to the good memories I had of my brother. We spent the day running around like children: playing tag, swinging, and playing in the sandbox. I know it sounds lame, but it was exactly what I needed. It was fun and freeing at the same time. I no longer felt like I had the world on my shoulders or chains around my ankles. Like a child, I felt free. I had no concern of what my next steps would be or worry about life in general. There was just us; me and Louie, being carefree and having the time of our lives.

He was worried for the first few days after, thinking I would close myself off and shut everyone out. But I was done with being alone. I had people here that cared about me, thought of me as family. They are all I have now.

We talked about the letter and what it revealed. I cried and got angry, but not like I was before. I was no longer angry at my brother, but at the foster father we had and the hand life dealt us.

And we also talked about Rayanne.

My brother was right; I didn't really know her. Looking back now, I realize I barely even remember what she looked like. I can't believe I was so caught up in my own misery and trying to stay in the shadows myself that I don't have one memory of her—of what she looked like or what her voice sounded like. She was three years younger than Hendrix and I. She didn't even live, yet she had lived through things that most people couldn't even imagine. She was good and innocent, but she was also a fighter and so very strong.

"Good morning, babe. What's got you thinking so hard?" Louie says as he squeezes his arms that are wrapped around my waist.

Rolling over so I'm facing him, I look at his sleep riddled hair and his lazy smile.

"I was thinking about my brother and Rayanne."

His smile turns sad. "Want to talk about it?"

Leaning forward, I plant a soft kiss on his lips. "I want to buy plaques for them. Hold a service. I never had one for Hendrix after I found out about his death and Rayanne never had a family. I don't even know what was done with her body," I say sadly.

Thinking back to those first few days after Hendrix and I left all those years ago, I remember the sadness that surrounded him. I foolishly thought it was despair for not knowing what we would do and being alone on the streets. I thought it was all the responsibility he took upon himself to support us. But now I know better. Now I know he grieving for the girl he loved and lost.

"I think that's a great idea. And it will help give you some closure." Louie speaks with sadness, but also with hope. I know he's worried about me, but it's because of him I have the courage to do this. It's because of *him* I'm finally on the right path to healing and getting over what happened.

"Thank you," I say as stare into his eyes. He has no idea what he's done for me. For two years I held on to my anger for what my brother did, thinking he was selfish and weak. I hated him for what he did. But now, with Louie and the club by my side, I'm finally on the road to healing.

"For what, babe?" he asks.

"You never gave up on me. Even after I left and was gone for so long. After coming back here the way I did and the way I treated you and everyone else I care about. But most of all, thank you for helping me through my anger and pain. For helping me see past it all and remember the good memories I have of my brother."

Louie rolls over so he is covering my body with his, then he kisses my lips. "I would do anything for you, Harlow."

No more words are spoken as nothing else is needed to be said in this moment.

He takes my lips in a rough kiss, but I meet his desperation with my own. We haven't had sex since the morning before he read me my letter. Going without him inside of me makes me ravenous for him.

"I need you inside me, Louie. I can't wait," I say, ripping my lips away from his, but not for long.

Attacking his mouth once more, I reach down to pull his boxers off, only to find he's already naked. *When did that happen?* Not wanting to waste time asking, I take his cock in my hand. He's so hard, I wonder if it's painful for him.

Not even bothering to take my own panties off, I move them to the side and eagerly feed his cock into my greedy pussy.

"Fuck," Louie groans as he pushes all the way inside of me.

He barely gives me time to adjust before he's thrusting viciously, but I don't care. The pain only adds to my pleasure.

"Faster, Louie," I urge him on. I can feel myself already at the brink of climax and I want it now. I need that orgasm more than I need my next breath. I'm desperate for it.

Picking up the pace, he doesn't disappoint. "Shit, Harlow. I'm not gonna last," he moans, but I don't care if this doesn't even last a minute. My whole body feels like a live bomb that's ready to explode.

"I don't care. Please. *Please…*" I beg him. I'm so close, I can taste it.

Lifting my leg for better leverage, he pumps into me harder, faster. With my leg now over his shoulder, he's able to hit a part inside me that sends shockwaves throughout my body.

"Oh, God!" I scream.

My orgasm starts to take hold, and just when I think I'll fall over the cliff into oblivion completely, Louie slows his pace a little.

"*No!*" I yell, thinking he's going to stop or make me wait. But instead, he delivers short, hard thrusts that has me seeing stars.

"Come with me, babe. Come *now!*" he growls before he stills inside me, but it's enough.

I scream out his name as I feel my whole body start to vibrate and contract.

After our breathing has settled and we're able to move our limbs, Louie lifts himself up so he's braced on his forearms above me.

"I think you wore my ass out," he says, still sounding breathless, but I think it's all for show.

"Oh yeah? Well, maybe next time you'll let me be on top." I give him a wink, then use all my weight to roll him over so I can straddle him.

He looks shocked, but turned on at the same time. "Oh no, you don't. I know that look. I have to be to work in twenty minutes, so unless you want to deal with Dani, I need to shower."

A part of me wants him to fight me, force me to stay in bed with him. But another part knows that we can't. I can't let Dani down after everything she's done for me. I was horrible to her when I got back into town. I owe her more than skipping work just so I can have more mind-numbing sex.

"All right, but your ass is mine tonight," he says, then he slaps my ass before tossing me off him. I give myself these few seconds to sit here and enjoy the view of him getting dressed before I make my way into the bathroom for a shower. A *cold* shower.

***

Louie left as soon as I was out of the shower, saying he had some business to attend to at the club. Grabbing my energy drink and phone off the counter, I head out the door. I've been staying in the apartment upstairs for the last couple of weeks, and even though I don't want to live here forever, I can't deny how much it makes things easier for me. Especially if Louie and I are going to make messing around minutes before I have to be to work more than a random occurrence.

Just as I reach the bottom of the stairs, my phone rings. Thinking it's Louie or Dani calling, I don't look at the caller ID before answering.

"Hello?"

Holding the phone between my ear and shoulder, I open the door to the back of the shop, but when no one replies, I stop. "Dani, is that you?" I ask.

Still, there's nothing.

"Louie, really? If you're fucking with me, I'm going to kick your ass when I see you tonight," I say with fake irritation. It gives me a thrill to have someone to mess with again. I haven't had this since I left here two years ago.

When I still don't hear a response, I pull the phone away from my ear to check the caller ID.

Unavailable.

"Hello? Who's there?" I try once more, and this time, I hear a faint chuckle, then the line goes dead.

Thinking it's just some kids prank calling, I forget about it and walk into the shop.

"Hey! Who were you talking to?" Dani asks as soon as she sees me.

"Hey, I have no idea. Probably some kids messing around," I reply as I head toward the front desk.

Sara is sitting at the desk talking on the phone, so I wait until she hangs up to give her a hug. "Hey. Married life still treating you well?" I ask in greeting.

When I got back and met Sara, I hated her. Well, I hated what I thought she represented. But getting to know her these past weeks, I realize she's kind of like me. And a lot like Dani. Which is probably the reason we are on our way to being really good friends, and not just co-workers.

I don't know what Sara was like when she first got into town, but I've heard stories and it seems like she's come a long way since then. I just hope that given time, things with me will be better as well.

"Married life is…sexy," she says dreamily.

"Ugh, please don't start telling me sex stories about you and Toby. I don't want the visual," I say jokingly. I would never deny her if she needed to let every detail out. I'm a good friend like that. What can I say, Toby is hot; they all are. So if their women want to talk about their sexy bodies and how they work their magic in the bedroom, I will lend an ear to listen. It's a horrible job, but someone has to do it.

"Well, if we can't talk about Sara and Toby's sex life, let's talk about you and Louie," Dani says from behind me.

Spinning around, I open to my mouth to lie to her about how Louie and I aren't together when the door chimes.

We all look to the guy who comes walking in with a large vase full of at least three dozen roses.

"Harlow McPherson?" he asks all three of us.

"Oh, that would be me," I say, confused.

As soon as I sign for the flowers, he hands them over and wishes us a good day. Making my way over to the desk, I set the vase down and look for a note within the masses.

"Who are they from?" Sara asks.

"I have no idea. There's no note," I finally say when I come up empty.

"I bet I know who sent them," Dani says cheekily.

"Oh shut up." To be honest, I can only think of one person who would send them, but I don't know why Louie would. I mean, we just saw each other mere minutes ago and it's not like we're really together. So why?

"No, but seriously, girl. Do you have something you want to tell us?" Dani asks in a serious tone.

"Nope. Nothing." It's the truth. There is nothing to say. Louie and I are friends who just so happen to enjoy each other's body on occasion. And we have strong feelings for each other, but it's still just friendship—with a little somethin' on the side.

Sure, I hope that it happens more often than every few weeks or just when the mood strikes, but that's me. We haven't talked about our relationship and I've been okay with that.

"Whatever, girl. You'll spill the beans soon enough, but until then, get your ass to work." I'm grateful that Dani is letting this go because I have no words. I've never gotten flowers before so I have no idea what this means.

Sitting down in the chair Sara vacated, I try to get into the mindset of work by going over the schedule and accounting books.

"Oh, I almost forgot. This was in the mail for you today," Sara says as she hands me an envelope.

I'm starting to get a bad feeling. This is all way too much for one day. First, my time spent with Louie. Then the phone call and flowers. Now this. What the fuck is going on?

"Thanks..." I let the sentence drift off, still trying to come up with a logical explanation. Things don't just happen like this, especially not to me. I don't get random calls. I don't get flowers. I don't get letters that I'm not expecting. And I *never* expect a letter.

"Well, aren't you just the popular girl today?" Dani says, though I can hear the edge in her voice. It's not directed toward me, but she is also a little weirded out by all of this. It's just too much. It does make me feel a little better that she feels it too though, and it's not just me.

Thankfully, she doesn't stick around to wait for me to open the letter. I don't want an audience because I have no clue what to expect.

129

Opening it slowly, I take a deep breath before reading the few words that are written in an unfamiliar hand.

My sweet Harlow,
It was so good to see you today. It's been too long. But soon enough that won't matter.
Until next time...
xoxo

I feel a chill go down my spine. I've had a feeling a few times that someone was watching me, but I wrote it off as being paranoid for no reason, or someone from the club following me. After Louie read me that letter from my brother, he's been really worried about me. And when he's not with me, he either sends me text messages to check up on me or he'll make sure I'm always with someone. I know he thinks I'll go off the deep end again, but I won't. Not because I'm over what happened, because I don't think someone can ever really gets over something like this, but because I don't *want* to. I have too many things in my life that are good, and I want to keep it that way.

But going off this letter, there is someone else out there, watching me, following me. And I have no idea who it could be. I don't know a lot of people around here. Only the people in the club or close acquaintances to the club. Of course there are the customers, but no one really sparks a thought that they would turn stalkerish.

Deciding there is no use thinking about it

anymore, I put the letter in my purse and get back to work. I just hope Dani doesn't ask me about the note. I don't want to mention anything till I have more time to figure it out. No sense worrying anyone unless it's necessary. It could just be some kid messing around, like the phone call. Although that doesn't seem likely.

***

It's late by the time Dani and I close the shop down. She had a last minute walk-in and I didn't want to leave her here alone to close. Plus, I didn't feel like going upstairs to an empty apartment.

Louie texted me a few hours ago saying he was still at the club, but that he would come over as soon as he was done. I haven't thanked him for the flowers yet, but I will. I just want to do it in person because I also want to talk about *us*.

I didn't want to get into it with him and try to label what we have, but after getting the flowers and the girls asking what's going on, I decided that I needed to know as well. I *want* to know. I really like Louie. I always have, but I need to know if this is more than just friends messing around. If that's all this is, that's fine, but I need to know. I don't want to be thinking this is going somewhere when it's really not. It may sting a little, but I'll take Louie any way I can get him. I don't want to live my life without him in it for another day I don't have to. And if that means only having him as a friend/booty call, then so be it. Like I said, I'll take what I can get, when I can get it.

"All right, you ready to head out?" Dani asks. She's been quiet tonight, more so than usual. It could just be me, or maybe she's still freaked out about the flowers and the letter, but I'm thinking it might be more than that.

"Hey. Is everything okay?" I ask. I haven't known how to get us back to where we were in our friendship before I left, but I miss her. If going by the way her face just dropped, I think she needs me as much as I need her.

"Not really, but there's nothing I can really do about it." Dropping down onto the sofa in the front room, she folds her legs up underneath her.

I'm still not used to this new, calm Dani. Before I left, she was headstrong and tough; unemotional sometimes. Now, she's sometimes unsure about herself and cautious. I like the changes, but I just need to get accustomed to it and figure out how to deal with her like this.

Sitting down beside her, I do my best to be the understanding friend. "What's going on? You can talk to me. I know I left and when I came back, I was frankly a bitch and horrible person, but I'm here for you. I hope you know that," I say.

"I know you are, babe, and I appreciate it. I really do. And I will talk to you about it, but not right now. I need to get my head around it first."

"I get it. You take all the time you need, but just know I'll be here whenever you need to talk. Or whenever you need to go out and have a few drinks. Lord knows it's been forever and a day since I've had a proper girl's night out with liquor. And I think we are *both* in need of that."

That has a smile on her face, which is exactly what I wanted. "Yeah, I think you're right. This weekend, you, me, and Sara. We're going out. No men, just us girls and as much alcohol as we can fit in our system."

Nodding, I stand and offer her my hand to pull her up. "It's a date."

CHAPTER 11

Louie

Today has been long but it was very productive.

Harlow mentioned this morning that she wanted to have a service for her brother and foster sister. I think it's a great idea. Not only do I think they deserve to have a service, but I also think it will give Harlow closure on what happened. She's come a long way in the past few weeks since finally reading the letter her brother wrote for her, but I think she still has a lot of healing left to do. And this may help, so I got together with a few of the guys at the club and we started planning.

We did some digging and found out that Rayann wasn't buried, but cremated. Since she had no family and the foster family didn't want to pay for a service, the state was forced to cremate her.

The good news is that her ashes were stored at a county office where unclaimed bodies are taken. We were able to get a release stating Harlow was family and that she would like to take possession of her ashes for a proper burial.

Mack agreed to let me send a prospect to retrieve the ashes. We haven't had any problems with a potential rival club, The Street Kings, that moved in a few towns over a couple of years ago, but we don't want to take the risk of sending a patched brother. If something were to happen, we need everyone on hand. Better to be safe than sorry, I guess.

So if everything goes according to plan, we should have Rayann's ashes within the week. And from what Harlow has told me, she has her brother's ashes with her, so we don't have to worry about that.

Next, I called around to see where there were two plots available side by side. I want them to be buried next to each other. Even though it will only be their ashes, or not, depending on what Harlow wants to do, I still think they need to be together. From the information Hendrix gave in his final letter to Harlow, he loved Rayanne and they were close. Whether by force or not, the facts remain the same.

Once that was taken care of, I made a call to a guy I know out in Nevada. He makes custom stone designs; anything from landscaping to headstones. He's actually the guy that I went to a few years after I came to California to do a headstone for my dad. He's the best there is on the west coast—if not in the whole US. I know he'll be the perfect person for what I want.

Pulling up to the shop, I notice a guy walking away from me. I have no idea who he is and don't want to chase him down because he could just be walking home from a bar for all I know but it's definitely strange. I'll be sure to keep my eyes open.

I check the lock on the back shop door before making my way upstairs to Harlow's apartment. I haven't spoken to her since the last time I texted her a few hours ago, but I hope she's still awake. I want to cash in on my threat from earlier.

Opening the door quietly, I see that all the lights are off in the living room, but the bathroom light is on and the door is cracked and the shower is running.

Being as quiet as I can, I make my way to the bathroom, stripping my clothes off on the way. When I'm inside the door, I have a clear line of sight into the shower, but Harlow hasn't noticed me yet. *Good.* I want to watch her without her knowing I'm here. I'm not a pervert, I promise. Or maybe I am, but only when it comes to her.

I watch as she rinses out her hair. Her eyes are closed and the way she moves while doing something so miniscule is also erotic. This woman is the sexiest girl I have ever laid eyes on.

After her hair is clean, she turns away from me to grab the body wash. Squirting some directly onto her hand, she starts by lathering it onto her arms, then moves to her chest. Seeing her touch herself has my cock harder than diamonds. Fuck, if she keeps this show up, I'm going to cum all over myself and the floor.

And of course, like she has a direct line to my brain, she doesn't stop there. After her breasts are covered with soap, her hands move slowly downward. It's like watching your favorite porn in slow motion. I hold my breath, waiting until her hand reaches its destination.

Not able to stand here any longer just being a spectator, I quickly make my way closer. Opening the door to the shower, I step in. "Was that show just for me, or do you always pleasure yourself while you shower?"

"Shit!" she screams.

I scared her so bad she jumped, which caused her to slip. Before she fell though, I quickly wrap my arms around her and pull her close to my body.

"You falling for me, babe?" I ask in a joking tone, though I do feel bad that I almost made her fall and hurt herself.

"*Goddammit*, Louie! You scared the crap outta me!" she yells as she tries to push away from me, but I don't let her. It was a long day being away from her, and then watching her in the shower, I can't stop touching her—holding her.

"Sorry."

"No you're not. If you were sorry, you wouldn't be smiling," she replies, but I can hear her own smile in her voice.

"Okay, you got me. I'm not sorry. I'd do it again if it meant having you in my arms, naked." Leaning down, I kiss up her neck and suck her earlobe into my mouth. Fuck, even her ear tastes good!

"Louie…" she lets her sentence trailer off. I have no idea if it's a plea to continue or stop, but she's not acting like she wants me to stop.

Moving one of my hands to her breast, I pinch her nipple. At the same time, my other hand travels down to the apex of her thighs where her pussy waits for me. Her pussy is wet, more so than it should be in a shower, so I know she wants this as much as I do.

Inserting two fingers, I feel her tighten her inner walls so I can barely move them. "Fuck," I groan, wishing it was my dick being clenched tightly instead of my fingers.

Picking up the pace, I thrust harder and faster with my fingers. Finding her G-spot, I massage it as I lean my head down to pull her nipple in my mouth while my other hand is still pinching her other.

"*Louie*," she breathes out, but this time I know it's a plea. She wants to come, and I want her to.

"Do you want to come all over my fingers, Harlow? Do you want to show me how much you love them inside this tight cunt?" I ask around her nipple.

"Yes! Louie, please," she begs. Even though I want to give her what she wants, I can't. Not yet.

Pulling my fingers out of her pussy, she sputters, confused why I stopped.

"You aren't going to cum unless it's around my cock," I say before moving my hands down to her ass, lifting her up. As soon as I slam her back against the wall, I'm balls deep inside her. It's a euphoric feeling being so close to her, so deep in her pussy that I can't even feel where I end and she begins.

Her sharp intake of breath has me worried I'm being too rough, but when her arms come around my neck and her nails dig into my back, I know she's not hurt. She may be a little pissed that I didn't let her come, but she's too far past the point she wants me to stop. She needs this release almost as bad as I need to give it to her.

"Fuck me, Louie. Fuck me hard," she moans, and who am I to not give her what she so desperately wants now that I have her where I want her?

"As you wish," I say, then I start thrusting harder and faster than I ever have in my life. I've never fucked a woman like this, and I don't intend to either, unless it's Harlow. I'll fuck Harlow like this every day, more than once a day, if that's what she wanted.

I feel her pussy getting tighter, so I know she's still so close to the edge of coming. I can also feel my balls start to tighten and feel heavy, but I don't want to come yet. I want to drag this out as long as I possibly can.

"Are you going to cum, Harlow?" I ask as I lift her higher, trying to penetrate her deeper and at a better angle. I can't wait to feel her come all over my cock. I just hope that when she does, I'm able to hold my pleasure back, even if only for a minute.

"Yes. *Yes*! I'm gonna cum, Louie. Please make me cum," she begs again and I know that if I can add more stimulation, she'll be falling over that edge quicker than she can take her next breath.

An idea strikes me. Removing one hand from holding her ass, I push her shoulders into the wall and pull my middle away from her a bit. "Stay just like that," I say.

Once I know she's not going to move, I reach up and grab the shower head. "What are you do—" she starts to ask, but before she can get the full sentence out, I direct the stream of water onto her clit as I continue to thrust inside her.

Her breathing ramps up and her pussy starts contracting, but not from an orgasm. More like lots of mini orgasms.

I noticed a few weeks ago that her shower head has different settings, so I use my thumb and forefinger to switch it to the harder, more pointed setting. It will deliver a smaller area of water, but it will have more force behind it. I want as much force as possible hitting her clit as I ram into her pussy. I want to give her the orgasm that will set the bar for all orgasms I give her in the future.

"Oh, shit. Oh, *fuck*!" she says, chanting it over and over again.

"Cum now, Harlow. Drench my cock with the pleasure only I can give you," I growl, needing to feel her cum just as much as I want to cum inside her. But I hold off.

It takes her a little longer than I thought, but a half minute later, her climax hits her hard. When she screams my name, it's a tortured scream, like the pleasure is killing her, but in a good way. At least, I hope it's in a good way, because I'm not done with her. Not yet.

I'm still inside her, waiting for her to calm down a bit. It kills me to not move, my balls aching and begging to cum, but I don't listen to them. They are just going to have to wait till I say it's time to take their pleasure from her body.

As soon as her breathing is back to a somewhat normal pace, I decide that I need to get her out of this shower. I want to lay her down and fuck her the way I need to fuck her, and it's not up against this shower wall.

Turning the water off, I step out of the shower with my hard cock still inside her. I don't even bother to grab towels for us. I couldn't care less that water will get on the floor.

"Whoa, what—" Harlow starts to protest, but I silence her with my mouth.

Once we're in her room, I lay her down roughly on her bed without breaking our connection. And I don't give her time to complain about her sheets getting wet or think about anything else, I just start to piston my hips at a punishing pace.

Long, hard, fast thrusts I deliver, wanting to make it so she feels me inside her body still for days to come. I want her to be sore and know that I was there. That her body is mine. And that I'm the only man capable of making her feel this way.

When I feel my orgasm coming on fast, I rip my lips away from hers. Grabbing her legs under her knees, I pin her to the bed so she's wide open for me. There is nothing she can do but take everything I give her.

"Fuck! Your pussy feels amazing," I growl, pushing even harder and faster into her. "Do you want me to cum? You want to feel my cum fill your pussy, Harlow?" I can already feel my cock start to twitch and jet cum inside her, whether she wants it or not.

"Yes. Yes, Louie, I want your cum!" she finally says.

Pumping into her a few more times, my orgasm

takes hold, starting at my lower back and spreading throughout my body.

It feels like it's hours before my cock stops twitching and her pussy wrings the last spurt of cum out of me. Falling onto her body worn out and tired, I lay there for a minute, basking in the afterglow of the best orgasm I've ever had.

Finally rolling over, I pull her body with me, situating her on top of me. It should be uncomfortable to have someone lay on top of you and sleep, but feeling her body on mine, knowing she's here, has me relaxing even more.

When sleep takes me, I come to the conclusion that this is how I want every night to end.

***

I wake up hours later feeling relaxed and happier than I can remember ever being. Things seem to be on the right track; Harlow is back, she's getting better, and things are good with the club.

It's then that I notice Harlow is no longer lying on top of me. Opening my eyes, I see her sitting up in bed, her back against the headboard.

"Hey. What are you doing up?" I ask. I'm still tired from the long day and our explosive sex session.

"What are we?" she asks in a small voice, though she doesn't sound upset.

Sitting up so our positions match, I look over at her. "What do you mean?"

"I mean, what are we to each other? Before I left, we were good friends who joked around and had a good time. We had sex and then I left before we were able to talk about it. Then, when I came back, things were messed up." She pauses for a moment, thinking over her next words. "Now, it seems we are jumping right back to where we left off, but I still have no idea what we are. Are we just friends, friends that mess around from time to time, or are we a thing? I have no idea what to think about us, Louie."

I'm not upset that she's asking these questions, because to be honest, I've thought about it too. But I haven't been able to put my finger on what it is I want out of this.

"Do we have to classify it?" I'm not trying to brush her off or hurt her feelings. I just honestly have no idea what we are or what I want. Come to think of it, I don't even know what *she* wants.

"What is it you want out of this, babe?" I ask. Maybe if she lets me in on what she's thinking, it will help me. But I honestly don't think we need to classify anything. We are what we are, and as long as we are both happy and willing, I don't think it should matter.

Harlow is quiet for a long moment, really thinking about what I said and what I asked. Then, she turns to me with a small smile on her face. It's not sad, it's content.

"No, Louie. We don't have to classify what we are or what we are doing here. I just didn't know how you felt, but honestly, I don't know what I want out of this either. I *can* tell you that I'm happy and enjoy spending time with you. And I also think the sex is awesome. So if you are okay not putting a title on what we are, then I am too," she answers and it leaves me with a huge smile on my face. Maybe I shouldn't feel triumphant, but I do. I feel like I'm on top of the world right now, and it's all because of her. Maybe that should tell me something, but for now I'm going to leave things be.

CHAPTER 12

Harlow

I feel better after my talk with Louie. Some may think that nothing was accomplished and the outcome wasn't good, but I'm not most people. What I got out of it was that he cares about me. That he's happy with me, even if it's not *classified*. And I'm happy too. Nobody else needs to understand. We are what we are, and that's fine with me.

Louie's lying in bed, talking on the phone. It's someone at the club, I'm sure of it, but I don't know who or what they're talking about. Louie's voice is quiet, but I'm not concerned. If it's club business, it's not *my* business. And if it's something that I need to be worried about or involved in, he'll tell me. I trust him.

Instead of staying in the room, I decide to give him his privacy.

Heading out into the kitchen, I start the coffee, but barely get the coffee grounds into the filter when Louie's yelling from the bedroom. "Harlow! Get your ass in here!"

I have no idea what jumped up his ass all of a sudden, but he doesn't sound angry at least. Finishing with the coffee, I decide he can wait a few seconds. Once I have the coffee pot on and it starts brewing, I pad back into the bedroom. He has a serious look on his face, but I know it's just for show.

"Yes?" I ask in a sweet voice and bat my eyelashes. It has the desired affect because he cracks a smile seconds before bursting out laughing.

When he settles down, he pats the bed. "Come here, babe."

Not moving, I cross my arms. "What for?"

"Because I'm not ready to share you with the world yet," he says this simply, like it's obvious.

I still haven't moved when his voice turns mocking, but with a deadly edge to it—a sexy edge. "Don't make me come get you, woman."

Finally, I move forward but stop at the side of the bed. I don't make a move to join him, wanting to see what he does.

I don't have to wait long. His hands strike out fast like a cobra, winding around my waist, pulling me into bed with him. Before I know it, his body covers mine and his lips come crashing down in a brutal kiss.

Louie thrusts against me, rubbing his hard bare cock against the outside of my panties, which causes me to wince. I'm sore.

Fuck, that sucks, but I guess I should have seen that coming. I lost my virginity to Louie two years ago, then went the whole time I was away without sex. Then I come back and after I finally let him back in, we're having sex. *Lots* of good sex. I mean, we aren't fucking like crazy by any means, but I've had more sex in the last two weeks than I have in my whole life. I'm gonna be sore.

Pulling my mouth free, I lift my hand and place it on his chest. "What's wrong?" he asks, concern lacing his face and tone, though I still see the lust and want in his eyes.

"I'm a little sore," I say shyly, a little embarrassed, but if we're going to have a sexual relationship, I can't hold anything back. And frankly, if I can talk dirty to him during the act and not feel embarrassed, I should be able to talk to him about things like this. It's normal I would be sore. Not only from not having a lot of sex in my life, but Louie isn't small by any means. Though I guess I don't have much to go off of, but I've seen pictures and porn before. And he's a lot bigger than what I've seen before.

He pulls back even further and looks a little lost and ashamed of himself for not going easy on me, or I don't know, thinking of it sooner. "It's fine. I'm okay, but I think maybe we should wait a bit before going at it again like wild animals." I try to smooth things over, but now I'm worried he'll be upset. Here he is, hard as a fucking rock, and I'm turning him down. Well, I'm turning him down for *sex*. But that doesn't mean—

"I'm such a fucking idiot. Harlow, I'm so sorry. I wasn't even thinking these last couple of times. I'm sorry," he says, and I hate that he's upset. He hasn't hurt me in any way and I loved everything we did together.

"Hey, it's fine, really. It's just, it's been a long time since I've had sex. I just need to get used to it." I add a wink to let him know that I want to have more sex with him, and soon, just not right now.

He still doesn't look convinced he didn't do anything wrong, but I'm done trying to explain it. Pushing him over so he's on his back, I straddle his waist.

"Just because I'm sore, doesn't mean we can't do other things, Louie," I say, then I lean down and start to kiss his neck. I slowly move down to his chest and by the time I'm at his bellybutton, he finally catches my drift.

"Babe, no. You don't have to do that. We can wait until you can enjoy yourself too." It's sweet of him to say that, but what he *doesn't* know is that I've always wanted to give him a blowjob.

When I first met him, I fantasized about it and the things I would do to him. The things I wanted to try. I even researched it and what men liked. So doing this for him now will be very enjoyable for me.

"I want to. *And* I'll enjoy it." I don't say anything else and move my mouth as quick as I can to his cock before he can argue the matter further.

He's not as hard as he was a few minutes ago, but he's still harder than what I'd imagine him being if he was limp.

The instant I have him in my mouth though, it's like an electric current runs through his cock and he's harder than ever before.

"Fuck," he moans.

I'm not able to take him completely in, but I add my hand at the base of him to make up for what my mouth can't fit.

Sliding my hand up and down, adding a few twists, I get into a rhythm. I lick the head of his cock before taking him as far as I can. Adding some suction, I then repeat the process. I take my other hand and massage his balls to add more stimulation.

Just as I'm starting to get into it and really enjoy myself though, I feel his balls tighten and his cock starts twitching before it goes even harder than it was when I started. I know he's about ready to cum, but I'm not ready for this to end. Not yet.

Slowing the movement of my mouth and the hand that's around his cock, I remove my other hand from his balls. Reaching up to my hair, I take out the hair tie I'm wearing so my hair falls down around me, all over his thighs. Louie either doesn't notice or he's so far gone in his pleasure because he doesn't act like he even cares or asks what I'm doing. *Good.* I want the element of surprise for what I'm about to do.

Without warning, I take the hair tie and wrap it around his balls. "*Shit*! What the fuck, Harlow?" Louie jumps a little, but I use both hands now to hold him down by his hips. If he really wanted to, he could get out from under me, but he doesn't. He's shocked, and might be a little uncomfortable, but he'll like what I'm doing in just a minute.

Once I know he's not going anywhere, I move one hand from his hips and tie the band tighter around his balls, but not too tight. Then I pick up my speed a little, sucking harder on his cock.

"Oh *fuck*," he moans, then the rest is a garbled mess of words.

Adding my hand back into the mix, I stroke him faster. "Harlow..." he says, trailing off.

Unwilling to stop what I'm doing to ask him what it is he wants or was going to say, I continue on. And every time I start to feel him get close to his climax, I slow back down and tighten the hair tie a bit. I'll let him cum, but in a minute. I want to see how far I can take this.

It's not much longer after that thought that Louie has had enough. Grabbing my head, he doesn't force me onto his cock, but he lets me know he needs to cum.

"*Faster*," he growls, and I obey.

I feel his balls get heavier and his cock gets bigger. When he's a few seconds away from coming, I remove the band quickly and then move my pointer finger toward his ass. As the first spurt of cum hits the back of my throat, I add just enough pressure to his anus to add that extra kick of stimulation, but it's enough. More cum floods my mouth and Louie roars out my name.

"HARLOW!"

His cum is never ending, so I have to swallow a few times to make sure I don't choke on it. Since I've never given a blowjob before, I wasn't sure if I would swallow or not, but it just seemed right. And it's not as bad as some girls have said. His cum tastes salty and bitter, and is almost hot going down my throat.

I swallow the last of his cum, then suck once

more on his softening cock, which jolts him a bit. "Fuck, babe. Don't do that," he says, though his words aren't harsh. I'm fairly certain it's because he's really sensitive right now.

Kissing the tip of his cock, I lean back and look at him. He's lying on my bed limply, his eyes barely open.

When he recovers a bit, he grabs my arm and pulls me down to him. He kisses me earnestly on the lips, then pulls back. A satisfied smile graces his lips.

"Holy *fuck*, babe. That was incredible. I don't think I've ever cum that hard in my life," he says, sounding completely surprised, but almost giddy like he wants to try that again.

I laugh, then lay my head on his chest.

We stay like that for a few minutes, then he asks, "What was that thing you did with your hair thingy?"

The question has me laughing, but also a little proud because I know what my answer is and know that it works. I'm insanely happy I did all that research now.

"I didn't want you to come yet, so I made sure you wouldn't," I say like I'm the President of the United States of America and just declared a law. I'm proud and demanding.

I've really shocked him though. He's speechless and looking at me blankly.

Finally, he replies, "Well, feel free to do that to me anytime."

I laugh, then close my eyes, content for the first time in forever.

***

An hour later, I still can't sleep, but that's okay. Carefully removing myself from Louie, I stand there and just stare at him. He looks so peaceful and damn good sleeping in my bed. The sheet is barely covering him; his left leg is completely uncovered, you can see his sexy V muscle on his stomach, and you can see his right hip but his leg is under the sheet. His one arm is stretched out, like he's unconsciously waiting for me to come back to him, and the other is reclined above his head.

I wish I could take a picture of him right now, so I could keep this image forever. I have no idea how long he'll want whatever it is we have going right now, but I know I'll want to look back on this time, years from now and remember how I felt in this moment.

Sighing quietly, I grab some clothes and head toward the bathroom. I showered last night, but then Louie dirtied me up again, so I figure I should probably get clean again before going in to work.

I notice the pot of coffee I forgot about earlier sitting untouched. Guess I won't have my caffeine fix before work.

Half an hour later, I'm showered and dressed. Louie still hasn't stirred and I don't want to wake him. He needs his sleep. I know he had a long day yesterday and who knows what he's been sleeping like before then, so I leave him to sleep.

When I walk into the shop, I hear Dani in her back office talking to someone, though I can't make out another voice, so maybe she's on the phone.

I don't intend to eavesdrop, but as I'm heading up front to my desk, I can't help but overhear her.

"You need to talk to him, Zane. There's something wrong, I just know it," I hear her say, but have no idea who or what she's talking about.

As I stop outside her door, I see her pacing inside her office. She hasn't noticed me yet and I'm not trying to hide either. I'm just concerned about her and wondering what she's talking about to Blaze. If something is going on, I want to know about it. Maybe I can even help. Lord knows I owe these people everything.

"I know he's a grown-ass man and he can handle himself, but there's something not right and he won't talk to me! Please, Zane, *please* just talk to him for me," she sounds frantic, which has my heart starting to race too. I wonder who she's talking about?

Dani stops her pacing suddenly, pulls her phone away from her face and looks at the screen. I don't know if another call is coming in or a text, but she stares at it for a minute before putting it back to her ear.

"Fine. Whatever," she says in a detached voice, then hangs up before I'm guessing he can reply.

I thought she would maybe start her pacing again, throw stuff, or yell. But she doesn't. She just stands there, staring off into space quietly.

Needing to know what's going on as much as I want to be there for her and make sure she's okay, I knock on the door to show my presence. "Hey, hon. I didn't mean to eavesdrop but I couldn't help but hear. Is everything okay?" I ask.

Turning around, she looks at me with helpless eyes. "No. It's not," she says, then walks over to her desk and falls into her chair like she's carrying the weight of fifty men on her shoulders and it's finally too much for her to bear. "It's Jax. I'm worried about him."

Jax was an old friend of Dani's from high school. They lost touch after everything that happened to her and she fled her hometown after graduation. From what I heard, he showed up at the shop a couple years ago looking for a tattoo and stumbled across Dani. After that, he just stuck around, prospected for the club, and is now a full member. I haven't spent a lot of time with him, so I wouldn't know if he's different or not, but I trust Dani. She would know and if she thinks there's something wrong, there probably is.

"Have you talked to him about it?" I ask, even though it's probably a stupid question. I heard her tell Blaze that he won't talk to her, but maybe she just meant that he *wouldn't* talk to her, not that she's *tried* and he won't.

She shakes her head. "Yeah, numerous times, actually. And every time I ask, he gets pissed off and says he's fine before stomping off to either the closest club whore or a bottle of whiskey."

"What about his behavior is off? I mean, what makes you think something's wrong?" I'm trying to help, but I can see the irritation in Dani's eyes and I don't want to piss her off. "I'm sorry. Never mind. It's not really my business." I turn toward the door, but Dani stops me.

"Harlow, wait. I'm not mad at you for asking,

I'm just mad at this whole fucking situation." I turn back to look at her and now the angry pacing that I was waiting for before starts. "But no one knows him the way I do. After Zane left for college, Jax and I got real close. He was like a brother and best friend all mixed into one. So when I say something isn't right, it's not just a stupid feeling or me being needy or whatever. It's because I know him and he's not right. Ever since he became a member, he's been off and I can't figure out why."

She's getting really upset now and I don't know what she'll do if she blows her top, so I try a different tactic. It will get her talking, hopefully lighten her mood, but it will also give me some insight as well. "I don't know him that well. I don't even think I've said more than ten words to him since I've been back because I didn't know him from before I left." I move toward the chair in front of her desk and take a seat, hoping she follow suit. "What was he like before he got patched in?"

Laughing, she walks back over to her chair and sits. "He was annoying, that's what he was. He always thought he had the answer to everything, and most times that answer was a party or getting drunk." We both laugh at that, then she's somber. "But he was also always there for me and never let me down. He cared about me and never let me forget it. I could always count on him for a smile or a shoulder to cry on."

I think about how she describes him and just from her words, I can tell they have an amazing friendship. I know why she's so upset over thinking there's something wrong with him. He's always been there for her, she just wants to be there for him.

"And now, he never smiles and barely talks. He's always angry and drunk. And from the blackness under his eyes, I can tell he's not sleeping. Something is *wrong*, Harlow. I just wish he'd talk to me about it. Let me be the shoulder for him like he always was for me." It must all finally be too much because she drops her head into her hands and starts to cry.

I make my way toward her and take her into my arms. "Shhh. It's okay. We'll figure it out, I promise."

CHAPTER 13

Louie

I hear a phone ringing off in the distance, but I don't want to wake up yet. I just want to lie here with Harlow all day and shut out the world. Last night was amazing and earlier this morning was even better. Not just because she gave me the best blowjob I think any man has ever gotten in the history of all mankind. Okay, well, that's not the *only* reason. But I felt like we really connected. Like she gave over a vital part of herself to me and me to her.

The phone goes silent, which makes me smile. Now I can go back to sleep with Harlow in my arms.

Reaching over to pull Harlow toward me because I need her closer, I realize that she's not even in bed. Snapping my eyes open, I see that it's probably about mid-day and that I'm alone inside the apartment. I don't see her in the bedroom and I don't hear her in the bathroom or kitchen.

Jumping out of bed, I rush toward my phone. The first thing I notice is that it's almost four in the afternoon. Way later than I originally thought. *Fuck*! I'm late for work. How did I sleep this long? I never sleep more than a few hours at a time, even when I've been up for days on end and tired as hell.

Picking up my pants that are still lying haphazardly on the floor where I threw them last night, I yank them on and pull my shirt on over my head. I don't even bother buttoning my pants before I'm out the door and heading down to the shop. I'm late and I know I need to get down there, but that's not what has a fire lit under my ass. It's because I know Harlow will be there and I need to put eyes on her. I fucking hate that I woke up without her next to me—without hearing her voice or feeling her body close to mine.

Pulling the door open harder than I probably needed to, it bangs against the wall, but I couldn't care less.

I head right toward the front of the shop because that's where I'll most likely find Harlow, but Dani stops me before I make it that far.

"Whoa, where's the fire, cowboy?" she says teasingly, but it's lacking her normal attitude. Hm, I wonder what's going on with her?

"Where's Harlow?" I ask, deciding to not get into what's got her looking down. I'll save that for another time, but right now, I need to see my girl.

"Of course you're here for Harlow. What was I *thinking* assuming that you were just hurrying because you were late for work?" This time her usual playfulness is present in her tone and eyes.

Ignoring her comment, I continue on toward the front room where Harlow should be and she doesn't disappoint.

But it's not just her that I see. There's a huge vase filled with dozens upon dozens of flowers. I don't know for sure if they are hers, but why else would they be on her desk? If Blaze had sent flowers to Dani, she would have them either in her office or at her station. And if Toby sent Sara flowers, which he's more apt to send them than Blaze, I doubt they would be sitting here when Sara is not.

Harlow looks up a few seconds later with a smile on her face, but it falters quickly. My face must speak of my confusion and quite honestly, my rage. But before she can ask me what's wrong or for me to question her about the flowers, my phone starts to vibrate in my pocket.

"What?" I ask, irritated by the interruption. I want to get to the bottom of who sent those fucking flowers to my fucking woman.

"Watch your tone, boy." Mack. *Shit.* "I'm calling church. Be here in ten," he says, then hangs up before I can say anything.

Hanging up the phone, I look at Harlow once more, then turn on my heels and run right into Dani.

"Now where you off to?" she asks.

"Mack called church. I gotta go. Have Harlow reschedule my appointments." I don't wait for her to comment and I don't look back to address Harlow herself. I just head out of the shop and jump on my bike.

Ten minutes later, I'm sitting around the table

with the rest of my brothers, but I'm finding it hard to focus on what could be going on that we were all called here out of the blue. We hold weekly meetings, but we haven't been called to an impromptu meeting for a while now. It must be something big for him send for all of us. Even the prospects are here. Of course, they're not allowed in this room, so they're out in the bar, but they'll get filled in after, I'm sure.

Once everyone is seated, Mack gets right to the point. "I got word today that The Street Kings have reinforcements. About five of their brothers from an out-of-town chapter showed up a few days ago. I don't know why they're here, but we need to find out. I don't want to be surprised by anything. If they are readying for something, I want to know about it. I want round the clock supervision on them and we need everyone here on alert. If this is going to turn ugly, I don't want to be caught with my pants down."

He looks around the room, making sure we are all taking this seriously and are all on point. As soon as he mentioned The Street Kings, all my rage from the flowers and Harlow got directed toward them. If they are up to something or trying to fuck with us, they're going to be sorry.

"Any questions?" Mack asks, but no one questions him or his sources. "Louie, Blaze, Toby, and Tom Tom. My office to discuss strategy. Slayer, Jax, Tyke. I want you to take point with the rest of the brothers. I want at least three brothers close to them at all times. Keep tabs on their comings and goings. Report back to me with any sign of suspicion or trouble." He slams the gavel down hard on the table.

Everyone dispenses, knowing what they have to do and what needs to be done.

I follow Mack, Blaze, Toby, and Tom Tom into Mack's office. Since I'm the last one in, I close the door behind me, then lean up against it with my arms crossed.

"What's your feelings on this? You think they're preparing to go to war with us or are they just bringing brothers in for the fuck of it?" Toby is the first to ask a question.

Mack sits down behind his desk and steeples his fingers in front of his mouth, thinking.

"I honestly have no idea what to think of this, and that's what worries me. I am completely in the dark on this one. When we got word that they first moved in, we heard all kinds of rumors and stories of their reputation. But we kept a close eye on them sonsabitches for a year and we saw *nothing*. We pulled back a bit, still watching, but *still*, we see nothing. Now, they're bringing more fuckers in? For what?" he asks, but it's a rhetorical question. He's thinking out loud while the rest of us are thinking the same thing in our heads.

"Could it just be a celebration?" Tom Tom asks, but he doesn't sound like he even believes it himself.

"For what? And why now? It just doesn't make sense." Blaze is the one to answer, but Mack nods in agreement.

"What have their business dealings been? Maybe something big is going down but it has nothing to do with us." This comes from Tom Tom again.

We each think that over, but that still doesn't sound right. "Nah, it's something else." This time, I'm the one to answer. "Mack's right, we need to keep a closer eye on them. Until we know more, there's no telling what they're up to."

"Make sure the girls are protected at all costs. I don't want any of this spilling over to them. Not this time. They've each been through too much," Mack says to Toby, Blaze, and myself. I've let them in on what happened with Harlow, and even though she hasn't been hurt or brought into anything because of the club, I'm glad they feel like she needs protection as well. She's one of us no matter how deep she's in.

"No fucking problem," Toby says.

"Maybe we should get the girls outta town this time. Send a prospect with them and have all three of 'em go to one of our safe houses with the kids." This comes from Blaze. He's being levelheaded right now, but I can see the fire in his eyes. If Dani doesn't agree to go willingly, he'll haul her ass somewhere out of the way kickin' and screamin'. She's been involved in the last few threats we've had, and been hurt every time in some way.

"I think that's a great idea, but will she go for it?" Mack asks.

Everyone is quiet, thinking about the way Dani would react. Everything is so up in the air with her most times, we never know if she's going to be reasonable or not. But this time, I think she will. I hate that I won't have Harlow here and be able to protect her if need be, but I know she'll be safer this way.

"She has the kids now. I think she'll be agreeable if we approach it the right way. And with the other girls going, she'll go no problem," I say.

Blaze looks at me, trying to read if I really believe that or not. And I do. "You're right. Maybe you should be the one to broach the subject."

I want to joke and give him shit that he's scared of his woman and too pussy to tell her himself, but I think he's right. I might be the best person to lay it all out there without sugarcoating it, but to also get her to see that it's the best option.

"All right man. I gotta get back to the shop anyway. I'll talk to her then."

Slapping me on the back, he says, "Thanks, brother."

I take my time getting back to the shop. As much as I want to focus on Harlow and the flowers, I can't because getting Dani on board is going to be tricky. I'm going to have to word what I say just right to get her to agree. And once I have her in agreement, the other girls will have no choice but to go along with her.

I park my bike and take a deep breath. Ready or not, this is going to happen. I only hope that it turns out the way we need it to. The girls *have* to be safe. The kids *need* to be safe. We need to know they are taken care of so we can focus on what is important here and that's getting to the bottom of what The Street Kings have planned and if it involves us.

I spot Dani first, but Harlow comes around the corner seconds later. Ignoring her, I grab Dani's hand and start to pull her toward her office. "What the fuck, Louie?"

Probably not the best way to get her alone so I can talk to her, but oh well.

As soon as we're in her office, I close the door on a confused Harlow.

"What the hell has gotten into you?" Dani asks, arms crossed.

I don't answer, still trying to get my words straight in my head. "I'm sorry, but I needed to talk to you alone." It's the only thing that comes to mind off hand.

Still standing with her arms crossed, she levels a glare at me. "All right. Well, you got me alone. Now care to share what the fuck is going on?"

What the fuck was I thinking? There's no easy way to tell her this or get her to agree to it, so I mind as well just spit it out and deal with it. Whether she likes it or not, she's going to the safe house.

"There's something brewing. We don't know what it is or what it means, but it could get bloody. You need to go home, pack up some clothes for you and the kids, and get out of town. We're going to have a prospect go with you, the twins, and the girls to a safe house. Until we can figure this out, it will be the safest place for you all." There. Just like that it's done. Now I just wait for the yelling or her to start throwing shit. Then I'll break it down further for her. Anything to make sure she gets what's at stake here.

But she doesn't do either of those things. She doesn't yell and she doesn't throw shit. She's not even looking at me like she wants to set me on fire.

"Did you hear me, Dani? You need to leave. It's not safe for you here." How can I make it clearer? I don't want to have to tell her all the ways she and the twins could be hurt, or worse, but I will if that's what it will take to get her to leave.

She finally answers. "I heard you." That's all she says. She doesn't agree with me, tell me she'll go, or tell me that I'm out of my mind. *Nothing*.

"You heard me? And you aren't going to argue?" It's crazy how much both she and Blaze have changed since the twins were born. I honestly can't tell if I like it or not, but right now, I think it's the latter. At least when she was bitching and fighting us tooth and nail, I knew what she was thinking. But now? I have no fucking clue.

"Yes, I heard you. And no, I'm not going to argue. You're right. If something is going down, I need to get EJ and Harley and take them someplace safe," she says, which has me speechless. That was easy. Almost *too* easy.

"But…?" I start, waiting for her to drop the bomb that has to be there.

"But nothing. Am I upset? Yes. Do I want to leave? No. But it's the right thing to do. I know that you're waiting for me to argue, but I'm not going to. Those kids are the most important thing to me. If this is what I need to do to keep them safe, then so be it."

Letting out the breath I was holding, I finally start to relax. I was ready to fight with her, but now that I know that's not going to happen, I'm relieved. I hate fighting with Dani and demanding her to do things. She such a strong person and I always want her to be in control, but in times like this, we don't have a choice.

I close the distance between us and take her in my arms. "Good. I'm glad you agree," I say quietly into her hair.

We stand like that for a few moments, then I hear her sigh. "But—" she starts to say, but I don't let her finish. Stepping angrily away from her, I throw my hands up in the air.

"Are you fucking kidding me right now? Of course you're going to argue. It's what you do best, Dani. But please. *Please* tell me what the fuck you have to argue, huh? You just said that your kids are the most important thing to you. And I just told you that they're in danger. Now you want to fight with me about this?" I ask, pissed that this is the way it's going to go. I should have fucking known.

She opens her mouth to reply, but I continue yelling. "Do you understand that they could take *you* to get to *us*? Do you get that? And not only you, but EJ and Harley! They could kill you, Dani! You, and EJ, and Harley. You'll all be fucking dead, and it'll be because of your stupid, headstrong ass." I know I'm being an ass and I didn't need to break it down like that, but maybe I did. She's always gotta argue, and look what always happens. Someone gets hurt or worse, they die.

"Fuck you, Louie. If you would stop being a fucking prick for one goddamn second and let me finish, I was just going to say but I don't want to close the shop. I need and want the kids safe and I know I need to be safe for them as well, but this shop means a lot to me too. So I was going to say

166

that I needed you to tell me that you'd still work. Keep things up around here until it's safe for me to come back. But I guess that's just too fucking much to ask, isn't it?"

Fuck. She's right. I *am* an ass. I just jumped right to the worst, thinking she'd never got for it and fight till the end to get what she wanted. And I was wrong. Seems I've been wrong about a lot of things lately.

"Shit, Dani. I'm sorry. It's just with everything going on and the position it's put everyone in, I jumped the gun. I'm sorry."

Again, she surprises me by calming right down and is understanding. The old Dani would have ripped me a new asshole 'til she was blue in the face. My outburst would have caused her to fight harder, but not now. "It's fine, Louie. I get it. Everyone is jumpy and all out of sorts I'm sure. But I'm serious. I need you here, at the shop, for as long as possible until I can get back here. I don't want to close it down for an unknown amount of time. It will kill our business."

"Of course I'll keep the shop open. You don't even need to ask. I know how much this place means to you and it means just as much to me. It won't be easy with having to handle everything from tattooing to the scheduling and paperwork, but I can manage. I can do this one thing for you so you don't have to worry," I say, and it's true. She's making a huge sacrifice by agreeing to leave so she's safe for us to do what we need to. I can do this for her.

Before she can answer me, the door opens and

Harlow is standing there with a look I don't quite recognize. "He won't have to do it alone. I'll stay behind and help."

Dani and I both look at her like she's outta her mind. Of course she can't stay back. She needs to go with Dani, the kids, and Sara so she's safe as well.

"No. Absolutely fucking not. You're going with her and this kids. Sara's going too. End of discussion," I say, drawing the line.

"*Not* end of discussion, jackass. You don't make decisions for me. I will decide what I do and don't do, and I decided that I'm *staying*. No one knows me or that I'm connected to the club. And it's the least I can do for Dani after everything she's done for me." I know she thinks she owes Dani and the club for bringing her in and helping her when she needed it, but she's wrong. We're family and that's what we do. We don't need thanks or to be paid back.

"I can't ask you to do that, Low. You need to come with us. We don't know what's going on or who we are dealing with. For all we know, they've been watching the shop. They'd know you are connected to the club, to me...to Louie. They could hurt you." Dani says, taking Harlow's hand in hers.

"You aren't asking, Dani. And neither am I. I'm staying and that's final. If they know I'm with the club and want to hurt me to get to them, then so be it. Everyone has made sacrifices. It's my turn now."

Insufferable woman! "Harlow—" I start, but she cuts me off.

"I'm staying," she says, then stomps out of the

room.

Great. Just fucking great.

CHAPTER 14

Harlow

As I make my way back to my desk, leaving both Dani and Louie behind in the office, I think back to what I heard.

I don't have any specifics, but I got the gist of it; something's happening that could be dangerous and they want the women and children to go into hiding at a safe house. But when it comes down to it, that's all I really need to know. That doesn't mean that I'm going to follow along though.

I do agree with Louie about Dani, the twins, and Sara going though. They each have a deeper connection to the club. Sara is married to Toby and Dani has children with Blaze. Me, on the other hand, I'm pretty much nothing to them. I'm an employee, slash friend, slash fuck buddy. I'm not trying to degrade myself or have a pity party, that's just the cold hard truth. And I'm okay with that. I'm content with it, too. But that doesn't mean that I'm going to run off at the first sign of trouble.

Dani and Sara have both been in sticky positions before I got back; each being hurt and put into danger. They don't need that again.

And knowing that Dani wants to keep the shop open gives me another reason to stay behind. I owe her so much. I can stay behind and make sure that all runs smoothly and help Louie out around here till things calm down and the girls can come back.

"You're going," I hear Louie say behind me, anger evident in his voice. I know he's probably upset about me staying behind, but I also know that that's not the only thing he's upset about. I could tell before he left to go to his meeting that he was upset about something. I just have no idea what it could be. Surely he's not mad because I left him sleeping in my bed this morning. Or maybe seeing the flowers, he remembered I never thanked him for them. Maybe he thinks I think someone else sent them?

"No I'm not, Louie. I'm staying here." I'm not going to let him railroad me into leaving when there's probably no threat anyway. At least not to me. But if there was, it's more important that Dani and Sara be gone with the kids, not me. And if trouble does come knocking, then I can take care of myself or I could even leave when it's a given that I need to.

I don't know what part of what I said did it, but Louie's eyes flash and I see something that I never want to see again directed at me: pure rage. It's so intense, it's almost demonic.

"Of course you don't want to leave. You probably want to stay here so you can keep fucking whoever it is that left you those flowers! Even if it means someone will take you, probably torture and rape you, before killing you."

His words have me completely speechless. I can't believe any of that came out of his mouth. First he accuses me of fucking someone because of the flowers I thought were from him. Then he thinks that even if that *were* the case, that I'd put my life in jeopardy to get my rocks off. And then lastly, the part about someone taking me, torturing me, raping me, and then killing me. How could he even say that shit to me? Any of it?

I try to talk, to tell him that the flowers were supposed to be from him, that I'm not messing around on him—whether we are exclusive or not, I would never have sexual relationships with more than one person at a time—and then tell him that what he said about me dying and how it would happen was totally uncalled for. But I can't get the words to come out. Not even a squeak pushes past my lips. *Nothing.*

"Oh fuck this shit. It ain't worth it," he says in a hate-filled voice before stomping off and out of the door.

I can do nothing but stare blankly after him. I don't cry or get mad. I'm cold and numb on the inside. Not even Dani walking up to me and taking me into her arms penetrates through.

Dani tries her best to get me to talk about what just happened, but I still haven't managed to even say one word. My mind is running a hundred miles a minute and I can't get the look on Louie's face out of my mind's eye. He looked at me like he loathed me, like he couldn't care less if all of those horrible things did in fact happen to me. There was no caring or compassion in his eyes. It was like the devil looking at me with rage and contempt. It makes me go back to a place I never wanted to go again. A place where I had no one and I didn't matter. I *hate* that place.

About an hour later, Dani comes walking out of her office. I think I heard her mention that she was going to call all the appointments for the rest of the day and reschedule or something like that. Now, she's just standing in front of my desk with what looks like pity in her eyes.

"Hey," she says softly, trying to smile at me, but even she can't bring herself to do that with what happened.

I don't answer her but I try to pay attention because I know she came out here to tell me something. Most likely important, but I just can't think about anything else except what Louie said and how he looked at me.

"Blaze wants me to get home so I can pack and get the kids ready to go." She pauses, then steps forward, like she wants to take my hand or pull me in for a hug, but she doesn't. I probably wouldn't be able to feel it even if she did, I'm so numb. "I really think you should come with me, Low. It'll be safer for you and will put all the guys at ease knowing they don't have to worry about us. *Please* say you'll change your mind?" Worry laces her every word.

I hate that I'm making her worry, but I'm not going. If anything, this just hardens my resolve to stay. I know Dani and Sara care about me, and probably a few of the brothers because they know I'm friends with the other girls, but I have no one I really need to stay safe for. If something were to happen to me, sure they'd be upset, but they wouldn't be devastated like they would if it were Dani, or the twins, or Sara. They'd be able to get over it if I got hurt. Or worse, everything that Louie described happened.

"No, Dani. I'm sorry, but I'm not going. I have no reason to. Plus, you need me here. So you go on ahead to get the twins and yourself ready, and I'll close up shop. Just promise to call or text me when you get to wherever it is you are going so I know you all made it there okay." I hope she won't argue with me further. I just want to close everything down here and go upstairs to hide under my covers. I want to shut the world out and just be by myself.

She lets out a sigh, then pulls me in for a hug. "You're so stubborn, Low. And you're so very wrong. You have every reason to go, even if it's for yourself. But I understand why you don't want to go, the *real* reason, even if you don't want to acknowledge it. Please be safe though. Don't take any risks and keep an eye out, okay?

Nodding my head, I hug her back. "I won't, I promise. The first sign of trouble, and I'm outta here," I say, though I don't know if that's a lie or not. A part of me really doesn't care what happens to me.

Pulling away from me, she looks at me once more before she heads out the door. Locking it behind her, I head to the back to lock that door before getting to work closing everything down. I finish the little bit of paperwork we have, clean both stations and the front room, then turn all the lights off.

Opening the door to the back, I lock it before making my way to the door that will lead me up to my apartment, to my temporary sanctuary, but a noise down the alley stops me in my tracks.

My heart starts racing, but I scold myself. Damn Louie for freaking me out like that. It's probably a cat or something.

I turn around to repress my fears but my eyes don't land on a cat. There's a man just standing there, looking at me. It's too dark to make out his face, but I get a weird feeling like I know him. But that can't be right, can it?

I take a hesitant step back to see what he'll do. Maybe he'll just stand there or turn around. But he doesn't. As soon as my foot lands behind me, he starts moving forward—he's not running, but he's walking with determination. Like he's trying to get to me.

Quickly turning around, I hurry to my door and fumble with my keys. *Come on. Come on!* I silently yell to myself. I can't believe this is happening to me right now.

Finally finding the right key, I hurry to unlock the door, then sprint up the stairs. Once I'm at the top, I look back, and see the door almost closed behind me. Shit! I can't believe I didn't close it all the way!

Just before the door slams shut and automatically locks, a hand reaches in to keep in open. *Oh my God!*

Running down to my door, I unlock it, then close it quickly before throwing the deadbolt. Stepping a few feet away, I stand there quietly, listening for anything that will tell me if that guy followed me up here or not. But I hear nothing. I don't hear a door shutting, any footsteps, or hear his voice.

A few minutes pass with me not moving. I barely even breathe. I wait and listen, praying that it was nothing. That the guy didn't follow me and that everything will be okay. Maybe he was just trying to scare me. Or maybe someone stopped him before he could make it up the stairs.

When I still don't hear anything, I start to relax. My whole body feels stiff and is starting to hurt with being so tense, but that's nothing a long hot shower won't cure.

Turning on my heels, I start to make my way to the bathroom when I hear the doorknob start to turn. Whipping around, I watch as it makes its way around, then stops when it meets the resistance of the lock. *Someone is trying to get into my apartment!*

Maybe once they realize they can't get in, they'll just go away. I still don't like it, but they can't get in here, right?

As soon as the thought hits me, I hear and see the doorknob start to wiggle. He's still trying to get in! And when that doesn't work, he starts hitting the door, like he is going to knock it to the ground.

I frantically look around my apartment for anything I can use or an escape, but I see nothing. My heart is racing and my mind isn't latching on to anything useful besides getting the hell out of here.

Forgetting about finding a weapon or a way out, I run toward the bathroom since that's the only door in here with a lock on it. Maybe if I lock myself in here and call for help, someone will be able to get to me before he does.

Pulling out my phone, I'm in such a rush to call someone and am shaking so badly that I drop it. "Goddammit!" I yell, then fall to my knees, searching for where it went.

I find it behind the toilet and am able to grab it quickly. I press the redial button, not even caring who it is, as long as they can help me.

"What?" I hear someone yell into the phone, and I'm barely able to recognize that it's Louie.

"Louie. Please help me," I whisper into the phone, trying to be as quiet as possible. I know it won't take long for the guy to figure out where I'm at once he gets into the apartment, but I need all the time I can get for someone to get here to help me.

"What's the matter, Harlow? Your flower fuck buddy can't come over so you need me to screw you?" he says with venom.

"Please help me, Louie. Someone is trying to break into my apartment. *Please*," I cry. I don't even care if he gets here only to yell at me and hate on me some more. As long as he helps me, I'll deal with everything else.

"Where are you?" he growls angrily, but I don't think the anger is directed at me this time.

"I locked myself in my bathroom. Please hurry, Louie. I'm so scared." I need to stop crying or else they'll hear me and know exactly where I am. It won't take them long to bust down this door too.

"I'm on my way, babe. Just stay with me, okay?" I can hear his bike start and even if I could, I wouldn't hang up on him. I need this connection or else I'll feel completely alone. At least with him on the phone, I know that he's coming for me and will save me. It doesn't matter if he hates me or never wants to talk to me after this, he'll come to help.

Just then, I hear a loud crash and I scream. "Harlow!" Louie yells into the phone but I can't concentrate on that. I can hear the intruder walking into my apartment, looking for me. It's too late. There's no way Louie will get here in time.

"HARLOW! Answer me, babe. What's going on?"

"He's inside. He kicked the door in," I whisper, though I know it's no use. This apartment isn't that big and this is the only locked door. He'll figure it out that I'm hiding in here and then it will be game over.

"Listen to me. Grab whatever you can find to use to protect yourself. I'm on my way, Harlow. Just hang on. I'm almost there," he yells over the roar of his bike and I believe him. He's on his way, but it's still not enough. He won't make it.

I see the doorknob to the bathroom start to turn and I hold my breath. I can't move and I can't speak. I want to tell Louie that I'm sorry for whatever it is that I did to make him hate me. I want to tell him that I'm sorry for not listening to him and Dani earlier. I should have left. I should have followed Dani and Sara and stayed safe.

Then I hear a bang, followed by a crash as the door is busted down, barely missing hitting me. And

I see him.

My whole body goes into overdrive and I drop the phone as I start backing away, but there's nowhere to go. I'm a caged animal and the predator was let in to feed. *There's no way out.*

The man has a mask on. He rushes toward me, trying to get his hands on me, but I start kicking with everything I've got. "No! *No!* Leave me alone!" I yell as I kick and hit, trying my best to make purchase, but it's no use.

He grabs a hold of my hair and yanks me to my feet. Still, I fight, even though I know it's futile. I'm not strong enough to fight him off, but I won't go down without a fight.

I'm able to hit him in the face. It's not hard enough to hurt him or slow him down, but it's enough to piss him off. His fist moves toward my face in slow motion and the only thing I can see is Louie's sad and angry face. I wish I could see him happy and smiling, even if only one more time.

Pain explodes across my face and I feel wetness run down my nose and I can taste it in my mouth. I fall backwards and hit the wall behind me. But the guy isn't done yet. I think he's going to hit me until I either pass out or he kills me. At this point, with the pain in my head, I think it could go either way.

"Please, don't. What do you want?" I plead, but I'm not expecting an answer.

Good thing I wasn't because this way I'm almost ready for the next blow. It hits me in the stomach.

I'm hunched over and can't breathe, the wind knocked out of me. I cry out in pain, but I wish I didn't because it just causes more agony to rip through my body.

I'm almost thankful when the next blow hits me in the face, on the same side as the first, and I start to notice black around the edges of my vision.

I'm getting lightheaded and feel my eyes closing, but it must not be fast enough for the man. He punches me once more in the face, and this time the only thing I can do is succumb to the blackness.

CHAPTER 15

Louie

I can hear her screaming and what sounds like a struggle. "Harlow! Please, babe, pick up the phone," I yell, hoping and praying she somehow is able to fight off whoever is hurting her, but the fight continues.

She cries out in pain once more, then there is nothing but silence. "Harlow. I'm coming, babe. I'm almost there," I say into the phone even though I know she can't hear me. I'm saying it more for myself than for her. I need to hold out hope that I'll make it there in time to save her and pray that when I do, she's still alive.

I don't hear anything else on the other end; no struggling, no talking, *nothing*. I don't know if the intruder left or what the hell he's doing, but I swear on my father's grave that I will find him and kill him. I will make him pay for every scream that came out of Harlow's mouth and every drop of blood that falls from her body.

My tires squeal as I whip around the last corner, then again as I skid to a stop in front of her stairs. Putting my phone in my pocket, I replace it with my gun. Looking around, I don't see anything out of the normal; no one is out here, there is no car, and there are no further signs of a struggle.

I want to rush up those stairs and burst into her apartment, but that's not the smart thing to do. If whoever was hurting her is still up there, I need to be as quiet as possible so I have the element of surprise. Then, I can be as loud as I want torturing him and making him pay. I'm going to kill him slowly and painfully, maybe even drag it out for a few days—*weeks* even—before I finally put him in the ground. Maybe I'll even bury him alive.

Creeping up the stairs quietly, I keep listening for anything that will give away what I'm about to walk into, but I hear nothing.

As soon as I'm at the top of the stairs, I see part of Harlow's door lying in the hallway.

Stepping over the pieces, still trying to be as quiet as possible, I look around the apartment. No one is in the kitchen or living room, so I make my way to the bathroom and what I see has me seeing red; and it's not all the blood I see smeared everywhere, it's from the rage running through my veins about what has happened. Someone broke into Harlow's apartment, hurt her so badly that there is so much blood I wonder if she's even still alive, and took her.

She's not here and neither is her captor.

"*Aaaggghhh!*" I yell, wanting to tear this apartment apart with the anger I feel running through me. *I* did this. *I* left her at the shop. *This is all my fault.*

Punching the mirror, I watch as it shatters and the pieces of glass fall into the sink and onto the floor. My hand is bleeding but I can't feel the pain. At least not in my hand. My heart is another story.

Blood drips from my hand and lands on the floor, mixing in with Harlow's. I wish it were all my blood. I wish I could take her place. She's hurt, probably scared, and no doubt hates me for not saving her. I wasn't fast enough, good enough, to be here to help her and now she's suffering because of me.

Falling to my knees, I give myself only a second to feel sorry for myself. To feel the pain that's lodged deep into my heart. "I'm so sorry, Harlow. But I promise you, I *will* find you and I *will* make them pay for what they did to you. I swear it, babe. If it's the last thing I do, I will save you." I bow my head and picture her in my arms and happy, not hurt or scared. Then, standing up, I put my game face on. I channel all the fear and pain I'm feeling and turn it into hate and rage. I shut everything off that makes me a man and focus on the part of me that I've repressed for so long; the monster inside me. I'll need him to do what needs to be done and I'll kill anyone who gets in my way. Harlow means more to me than my own life.

Pulling out my phone, I dial Mack. "Louie. You find something?" he asks, having no clue exactly what it is I found.

"Dani and Sara make it to the safe house?" I ask, needing to at least know they are okay before continuing on with what has to be done. I don't know what I'd do if Harlow wasn't the only one taken. But then again, if she was the one singled out, what does that mean for her?

"Yeah. Blaze just called and said they are getting them set up. Why, what's going on?" He doesn't sound worried yet, but his voice has gotten a little harder. *Good.* I'm going to need the ruthless, Mack. I need him to help me do whatever it takes to get Harlow back.

"Meet me at the shop. Bring whoever is available."

I hang up the phone without waiting around for his reply.

Looking around the apartment once more to see if there is anything I can use as a clue to find her, I then make my way downstairs to wait on my brothers. I can't be up here anymore. It will just bring the pain back and I can't let that happen. I need the cold hard monster that I have become to get through this and find my girl.

Once downstairs, I try the knob on the shop door to see if it's locked. I have no idea if Harlow was stalked inside here and chased upstairs or if it happened after she closed up, but being that she was able to lock this door, I would assume it happened after.

Taking a quick look around to verify nothing is out of place, I make my way toward the front. I start to go through all the paperwork from the last few weeks to see if I can see something that doesn't look right. Since I don't even have a starting place for who would take Harlow, I don't know if it was a customer or someone else.

I want to wait for my brothers to get here so I can see what we have on the rival club. I don't know if they are involved or not, but it would make sense. But why Harlow? They could have hit us in a million different places before setting their sights on her. So the fact that they didn't makes me think something else is at play.

In the distance, I hear bikes approaching which means Mack and the others are almost here and we'll be able to start figuring this shit out. The sooner we have a starting place, the closer I'll be to finding Harlow.

The bikes shut off and seconds later, the door opens and Mack rushes in with Tom Tom, Tyke, and Jax behind him.

"What's going on, Louie?" he asks with a hard edge in his voice, but it's not directed at me like he's irritated or pissed. He knows I wouldn't have asked him here if it wasn't important. And I wanted to wait till they were here before I told them, that way we could figure it out together.

"Harlow was taken," I say calmly, but I'm anything but calm. I just know that nothing will get done if I start raging and yelling at everyone. I need to hold myself together in order to get to her. Save the monster for the fucker who hurt her.

"What the fuck? What do you mean she was taken?" Mack roars, rage taking him over just like it did me.

"She called me. Said someone was trying to break into her apartment. I could hear him break the door down and there was a struggle. By the time I got here, it was too late; Harlow was gone and there was no sign of who took her."

Mack is pacing by now and it's Jax who starts asking questions. "Do you have an idea who did this?"

Shaking my head, I go back to what I was thinking before they got here. "I have no idea. I started going through some paperwork here to see if maybe it was someone who came into the shop, but I don't see anything out of the usual. The only people who have come in the past few weeks have been regular customers," I say, then I look at Tom Tom. "Do we have any new information about our little friends?" Maybe they'll know something new about The Street Kings and it will either condemn them to their fate or clear them of suspicion.

"No, nothing yet. The two prospects are hanging back, sitting on the clubhouse to see what they can gather, but they haven't seen any movement yet. No one has come or gone for the past few hours, but that could just mean they left before we got there and haven't come back, or they are holding her somewhere else."

"Do we have eyes on their warehouses and places of business? If it is The Street Kings, maybe they're holding her at one of those locations," Jax says.

"We don't have the manpower right now to cover that many locations. Blaze and Toby left with the kids and girls to get them situated. We're posting two prospects to guard them so they can come back. As soon as that happens, we should have enough guys to cover the clubhouse and other locations," Tom Tom says.

"Are we even sure that it's them? If it's someone else who has her, we'd be wasting our time while whoever *did* take her has free rein." Tyke speaks up for the first time. What he said pisses me off but he's also right. We don't know if it was The Street Kings, but it's our only lead right now.

"We're wasting time by you delaying our plan to check out the Kings! It's all we have right now. So we can either all sit on our thumbs trying to come up with all possible leads or we can *do* something; we can watch them or even rush in there and get answers by any means necessary," I say, done with all the questions. I can't just sit here and talk while she's out there with God only knows who and they are doing God knows what to her.

"Calm down, Louie. We're just trying to figure out the best course of action," Mack says, noticing that I'm about ready to lose my shit.

"The best course of fucking action would be to storm into their clubhouse and kill each and every one of those motherfuckers. Then we can search the place for Harlow, not stopping until we find her!" I roar, done discussing this.

Turning around, I make my way toward the back door to do just that when I feel a hand on my shoulder stopping me. Whipping around with my fist already in motion, I swing out and hit Mack right in the face.

"Don't you dare fucking stop me, Mack! I played by your rules last time, but we're doing it my way now! You hear me?" I yell, ready to hit him again if need be, President be damned.

When my father was killed, I did everything Mack told me. I was able to rein the monster in, at least a little, until the time came to unleash him. I can't do that this time. I can't hold myself back. Not with Harlow taken and hurt. If I have to go against my club to get her back, then so be it.

"I'm not telling you to stop! I'm telling you to hold the fuck up so we can do this the smart way. If they *do* have her and you go in there guns blazin', do you think they'll let her live? They'll *kill* her right fucking there! We need to be smart, Louie. I want her back just as much as you do, but we need to be together on this," Mack yells back, trying to talk sense into me. And I know he's right. I know that if I go in alone and unprepared, they'll just kill her, but I can't handle this shit. I need to be doing something, *anything*, to try and save her.

"I know what you're feeling and I know what you're doing. You're shutting everything down like you did years ago when your father was murdered. But you need to take back control. You need to let in more than just the rage, otherwise you'll risk losing yourself too. What good will you be to Harlow if you've lost all your humanity, huh?"

His words start to penetrate, but I still fight it. I hold on to the monster inside until I know I can do this without him.

Mack must see my inner struggle, but instead of continuing, he turns to my brothers who are standing there watching all this transpire. "Call Blaze and Toby, get them caught up and have them get their asses back here. Make sure they don't tell the girls. Then call Slayer to check in on the Kings.

Louie and I are going upstairs to see if we can find a lead. We'll meet back here in ten." With that said, Tom Tom, Tyke, and Jax take off outside to do his bidding and Mack pushes me out the door and up the stairs to Harlow's apartment.

I hesitate outside her door, not wanting to go inside and see the scene I saw earlier. It's too much and I'm afraid that if I go in there again, I will break down. I'll lose my carefully composed rage and it will turn into pain. I've never wanted to be a monster as much as I want to right now; as much as I *need* to right now.

"Quit being a pussy and get the fuck inside. *Now*," Mack says with all hardness in his voice.

"Fuck you," I growl, turning around to deck him again, but he catches my arm at the elbow by hooking his arm with mine, effectively stopping my punch.

"No, Louie. Fuck *you*," he says, then pushes me inside. "I know exactly what you're doing. You want all the pain and anger to drive you to find Harlow. I get it and I think that's what you need too. But you can't turn everything off. You need every one of your emotions to get this shit done. Without it, you're just a cold bastard that will probably get himself killed—if not others around you."

I want to yell and hit him, but part of what he says rings true, I'm just scared to admit it and even more scared to let the pain back in. There's a good chance I could lose Harlow tonight. And if that happens, I don't know if I can go on.

After my dad died, it was hard, but I never once

thought I couldn't go on without him. My revenge and Mack drove me on and I continued to live. It may have not been as full of a life as I would have wanted, or my dad would have wanted for me, but I lived.

This time is different though. Harlow has consumed me, body, mind, heart, and soul. I think I love her. No, I think I'm *in* love with her. So if she dies, if I'm too late to save her, I won't be able to live. And what's more, I won't want to.

"Son, listen to me. We are all here for you and I give you my word we will do whatever it takes to find Harlow. We'll tear the universe apart if that's what it takes to find her. But you need to put your faith in your brothers—in yourself. If you don't, then we might as well stop right now because the outcome won't be pretty."

I feel wetness sliding down my cheek and I know exactly what it is. I haven't cried since my dad died, and even then, I think those were more tears of rage. But the pain I feel for what's happened to Harlow—what is continuing to happen to Harlow as we speak—just crushes my heart. The girl I love was taken brutally and I wasn't there to save her. I once again put my wounded pride before someone I care about and once again, they are paying the price. And that truth hurts like a bitch.

"I'm scared, Mack," I whisper, dropping my head in shame. What he must think of me. I've always looked up to Mack and I owe him my life. Without him, I wouldn't have amounted to nothing after my dad died. Mack is like my second father. He didn't replace my real dad after he was murdered, but he filled a void that I thought would never be whole again.

"I know you are, son. We all are. But we'll get through this. *Together*," he says, then steps forward and wraps his arms around me. I'm man enough to say that it's exactly what I needed. And if anyone has a problem with it or wants to call me a pussy, I'll beat their fucking ass. Pussies are men that deny love and companionship; whether it's from a woman, a brother, or a father. Family—blood or not—is what's it's all about.

Pulling away, he slaps my back. "Now let's find our girl and put some men to ground; where they fucking belong."

CHAPTER 16

Harlow

Pain. That's the first thing that comes to my mind. I feel like I was literally run over by a train. Every part of me hurts; my toes, my legs and arms, my chest, face, and even my hair hurts. *What the fuck happened?*

Then it all comes back to me—the guy in the alley, running up the stairs and into my apartment. Locking the bathroom door and listening to the front door being kicked in. Then, there was the guy from the alley with a mask on, breaking into the bathroom and hitting me over and over and over again until I passed out.

The sound of movement to my right has my heart beating faster and my panic rising. Whoever is beside me is probably the man who took me and beat me last night.

I try to open my eyes, but can barely manage to open only one. The other must be swollen so badly or damaged because I can't see anything out of it.

I'm currently lying down, so I move my head to the right and sitting in a chair on the side of the bed is a man. But he's not a stranger to me; I've seen him before.

"Titus?" I ask, confused why he would be here. He can't be the man from last night.

"Good morning, sunshine." His voice is different. There's an edge to it now and I wonder if it were there the whole time and I just never noticed it before. The man I remember was funny and friendly. But that's not who's sitting beside me now, especially if he was the same man from last night.

Titus was the owner of a bar I worked at a few months ago. After my brother died, I couldn't stay in the house he killed himself in, but couldn't come back here either. So I became a nomad. I drove until I was out of gas and found small bars or restaurants to work at for cash. I'd sleep in my car or occasionally get a hotel room if the tips were really good that night.

Then, when the memories started creeping up, I'd pack up and leave without a word. I never looked at a map. I just drove down the highway, not looking at signs or thinking about where I was going. When I'd arrive at the next Podunk town, I'd repeat the process; working any job I could get until I had enough money to leave again or until the pain of my past was too much.

"What am I doing here?" I ask, trying to figure all this out but it's becoming more and more real to me. He's not the person I once knew, if I even knew him at all.

Thinking back on it now, I realize I don't know him at all. I was only in Nevada for a month, two at the most, before I decided to come back here. You can't get to know someone in that amount of time and it's not like we hung out or really talked. He greeted me a few times and we talked about unimportant things, but that's it. I never got to know him as a person, just assumed he was a normal guy and left it at that.

I didn't want to get to know anyone. I wasn't interested in dating or talking about where I was from or why I was running. I didn't want anyone to see what was behind my numb exterior. Shit, *I* didn't even want to see that. I closed myself off for so long, it just became second nature. So I don't know this man in front of me besides his name and that I worked for him at a bar. But now I can see that under that friendly façade is an evil and sadistic man.

Titus leans back in his chair and looks at me with contempt. "Well, sunshine, you're here because I want you to be here. And this time, I'm going to get what I want." He acts like his reply was answer enough and I should be able to fill in the blanks, but I can't. Or maybe it's just that I won't. I have an idea of what is really going on, but I'm scared to fully admit it because that would mean I'm in big trouble.

"Was that you in the mask last night?" I need to know for sure, even though I'm fairly certain it was him. Who else would it be? He's the only one here, as far as I can tell, and if it wasn't him, then why is he here now? No, it was most certainly him, but I still want to hear him say it.

"Yes," he says like he's answering a simple question like if he's hungry. How can he be so nonchalant like that? He hit me—*numerous times*—and took me from my home against my will. What he did is not okay! It is far from it.

Getting angry now, I sit up, but it's a chore. I think I may have a few broken ribs, or they're at least bruised, and my head pounds to the beat of my heart. But I push through the pain so I'm not lying down. I need to appear stronger and more in charge, otherwise he'll think me weak, even if I am at this moment.

"How dare you. What gives you the fucking right to kidnap me, you piece of shit?" I shouldn't goad him but I'm not going to cry and feel sorry for myself. I'm not going to lie down and let him do whatever he wants. If I do, he wins. And that is not going to happen. I don't care if I wind up with a dozen broken bones, I'm not going to let this happen. I will *fight* for my life. I'll defy the odds so I can get back to my family. Or die trying.

My words don't piss him off like I thought they would. Not like I'm complaining though, it's just messed up. He was so quick to beat the shit out of me last night when he took me, but not when I mouth off?

"I'll tell you what gives me the right, Harlow. It's *my* right because you're *mine*," he says.

When I try to argue the fact that I'm not his and never *will* be his, he cuts me off. "When you came into my bar looking for work, I knew right then that you would be mine. And I worked hard for it. But did you fuckin' notice? *No!* And then you *left* me? To come *here*?" Now he's getting angry. He stands up and starts pacing, shaking his head like he's having an internal battle inside his mind. *Shit, maybe he is!* He's fucking bat-shit crazy. He must be considering what he's done to me.

"I thought that maybe you'd need some time to warm up to the idea of what I am, but I can see that it wasn't necessary because you're already associated with the likes of me."

His words confused me. What does he mean by *the likes of me*?

Titus notices my confusion. A sinister smile overtakes his cruel face. "Oh yeah. I know that you're with the Sinners," he sneers. "And I've come to learn that you knew them before you came to me. You're *already* a biker whore."

I still don't follow, but I don't like where this is going. I'm not a whore, but I *am* associated with an MC. Does that mean…?

"I can see you piecing it together, but let me formally introduce myself. I'm Titus; President of The Street Kings—Nevada chapter."

The name doesn't ring a bell, but I know enough about bikers that it's not good. If he's the President of another MC, that means that chances are they are rivals of the Forsaken Sinners. If he knew I was with Louie or even if he just knew I was working for the club, he wouldn't have dared take me. He wouldn't have risked a war. Unless they are enemies.

Wait, though. He said the Nevada chapter. So what the hell is he doing here, so far out of his territory? And how did he find me in another state? Fuck, are we even still in California, or was he able to take me back to Nevada? *Shit!*

Then I think of something else.

"But the bar I worked at. It wasn't a biker bar. And you never wore a cut signifying you are a member." It doesn't make sense. If I've learned anything from being around the Sinners, it's pride over your colors. They wear their cut like a second skin and without fear of consequence. So if he is who he says he is, why wasn't he wearing his?

"And there's where you are wrong, sunshine. The bar's name was King's Bar. And we *did* wear our colors. You were just too caught up in your own head to notice. Probably thinking about your precious *Sinners*." He says their name with such contempt. I don't know if they have always been rivals or if it's new, but the way Titus speaks it's like they've been enemies for hundreds of years.

I try to think back to my time at the bar. I know it was King's Bar, but that didn't mean anything. It was just a name. How was I supposed to know it was a biker business? For the life of me, I can't recall ever seeing even *one* man wear a vest with their name on it.

Thinking harder, I close my eyes and try with everything I have to recall an image from a day I was there, but I come up empty. I can barely remember even talking to Titus or anyone else. I kept to myself and only spoke when I was spoken to directly, and most of the time it was just to take a drink order. How did I fuck this up so badly? How did I not know I was in the presence of another

MC? That I was *working* for one?

"The fact that you can't even remember shows how useless my efforts were! You barely even fucking remember *me*, let alone what club I belong to!" He stops pacing and faces me head on. The look in his eyes can only be described one way; manic.

Moving slowly so my feet are now on the floor to make my escape the first second the moment arises, I try another way out of this. "Titus, please. Just let me go home. We can talk about this. I'm sorry I don't remember much, but I was in a bad place. My brother had died and I was numb to everything and everyone. But if you let me go right now, we can get to know each other. I promise." Maybe the combination of my begging and telling him that if he lets me go we might be able to work something out will change his mind. Of course I don't intend of following through with any of it, but I'd say anything at this point to get me out of this situation. To get me away from him.

My words have no effect on him though—not even a twitch of his eye to let on that my words at least caused him *some* emotion.

"You really expect me to believe that if I let you go, you'll come to me *willingly*? That if I let you go you won't go running back to that club or that piece of shit you've been fucking?" My eyes go wide. He not only knows about my association with the club, but my relationship with Louie? He's been watching me. Waiting for the perfect time. He's probably the one who sent me those flowers and that note. And the strange phone call I got that day, that was him too. It's all falling into place now.

"No. You're not going anywhere. And this time, instead of asking, I think I'll just take." He lunges toward me, intent on pinning me to the bed.

The adrenaline overshadows the pain in my body and I'm able to dodge him. He must not have expected me to be able to move so quickly, but it's a mistake on his part I'm thankful for.

I'm able to make it out the door of the room I was in and halfway down the hall before I hear him coming after me.

I have no idea where I'm at. I'm not familiar with this place at all, which means I'm going to have a hard time getting out of here. I don't know if I should turn right or left at the end of the hall, so I'll just have to take my chances.

The hallway breaks off into what looks like a living room. I quickly glance to my right and see another hallway, but before I can turn to the left to go that way in hopes it will lead to the front door, something slams into my back.

Titus wraps his arms around me to hold me against him, but I twist and turn, trying to break his grip. I'm able to get one arm free, but the other is clasped in his hand.

"I said you aren't leaving!" he snarls at me, then yanks me toward him.

My front is to his front, so I raise my knee and try to kick him in the balls. If I can get a good hit on him, maybe he'll be in enough pain he'll release his hold on me, long enough that I can run. But he's able to block me easily as he twists me around to face him, proving that fighting him off isn't going to work. If I have any hopes of getting away, I need to find a weapon.

Something shiny catches my eye behind him. It looks like a Katana sword hanging on the wall. Looking back at Titus, I spit in his face, which causes one of his hands to let me go so he can wipe his eye. I'm able to break free from the other hand and get around him.

I'm almost to the wall when I'm grabbed from behind. Titus picks me up as if I'm a ragdoll so I'm at least a foot off the ground, then swings his body around.

Next thing I know, I'm flying through the air and falling down fast. My back hits something hard, but it gives to the weight of my body. *A table.* I landed on a table and the force was so hard, it broke underneath me.

The air is knocked out of me from the impact, but seeing Titus rush toward me doesn't give me any time to catch my breath or think of the pain I feel running up my back and into my head.

Flipping myself over, I scurry on my hands and knees away, but Titus grabs me by my ankle, dragging me back. "Come here, you little bitch," he yells while he pulls me toward him.

"No," I say, but I don't know if he heard me. It was more for myself anyway—to draw more strength to get away from him.

I try kicking my feet to hit him anywhere I can, but it's no use. He just grabs both feet and continues to drag me back. My arms flail out, trying to grab on to anything to stop myself from being pulled, when my hand lands on a piece of broken wood from the table I went through. Pulling it closer to me, I grab on to it with both hands. Turning my body around so I'm lying on my back, I swing the board across his face at the same time, using all the momentum I can gather from the move.

The sound of the wood hitting him hard in the head echoes in my ears. His head snaps to the side and blood starts to pour out of his nose, mouth, and a large gash where a sharp piece of the wood cut through his cheek.

"*Fuck!*" he roars, but it's garbled from the blood in his mouth and the pain he must be feeling.

I'm able to get to my feet, but from hitting the table and grappling on the ground, my sense of direction got messed up, so instead of heading the other way toward what I hoped was a door, I'm now heading toward the other hallway.

Too scared to turn around for fear that he'll catch me again, I continue making my way down the hall, looking for another weapon I can use against him or a side door.

I make it to the end of the hall and realize this was a dead end. The only thing back here is a bathroom. There are no other doors and nothing I can use against him. I'm trapped, *again*, in a bathroom.

Before I can turn around to see if Titus has recovered yet, he rams into my back. The momentum from the push causes me to fall into the bathroom, the sink catching my hip. "*Ah!*" I scream, the pain almost making me vomit.

My body is hunched over from the intensity of the pain. "You're going to fucking pay for that, bitch!" Titus growls from behind me, then grabs a handful of my hair, forcing my head back at an unnatural angle.

I don't have time to think or worry about what he's going to do to me now that he has me in his grasp again. It happens too fast and the next thing I know my head is being slammed into the mirror.

Glass rips through my forehead and wet, sticky warmth gushes into my eyes. I cry out and feel myself getting lightheaded. It's all become too much on my already broken and bruised body.

But he's not done yet. Hand still in my hair, he pulls me back.

Trying one last time to get away, I force myself forward, not even caring if I tear all of my hair out in the process.

I don't even loosen his hold a little, but he lets go on his own accord. I just wish it was because he was done with me. I'm not that lucky though. Grabbing me around my waist once more, he hurls me to the side, making me crash through the shower door.

Falling into a crumpled mess on the shower floor, shards of the tempered glass fall all around me. I feel cuts on my arms and side from when I went through the door, but as the bigger pieces fall down around me, one lodges itself into my leg, causing a bloodcurdling scream to rip out of my throat.

The last thing I hear is Titus laughing, then the smell of all my blood pooling around me fills my nose and the pain is too much to bear.

I send a silent prayer up to my brother to take the pain away. I pray that I'm dying so I don't have to open my eyes again to see the monster that took me away from the only family I had left.

I pray for death.

CHAPTER 17

Louie

It's been thirteen hours since Harlow was taken and they've been the longest hours of my life. It feels like an eternity since I last saw her and I hate that it wasn't seeing her happy, smiling.

I was such a prick to her, thinking she was fucking someone else. I've had enough time to think about it and know I was wrong. *So wrong*. She'd never do that. It doesn't matter if we are officially together or not, she wouldn't do that to me; to anyone. Harlow is so innocent and good, down to her very core, that it would hurt her more than it would hurt someone else to betray them like that. No, she's not like that. She wouldn't hurt anyone.

Me, on the other hand. I've fallen so far from where I need to be. I've never really been nice, but I'd like to think that if my life had been different— if I didn't grow up in a such a shitty town with shitty people—I would have been different. Or maybe that's just wishful thinking in a time as horrific as this.

But then again, if my father hadn't been murdered and we left like we were planning to, I *could have* been different. I could have been a good man, a man that deserves a woman like Harlow.

She's been through so much. First, not having any time with her real parents before they were ripped away from her. Growing up in the foster system, never knowing if the next home would be better or worse, and always wondering if there was something better out there. And then her brother taking his own life and finding out *why* he did it; what he went through and what he sacrificed to protect her.

Harlow deserves to be happy and get everything she ever wants out of this life. Right here, right now, I vow to give her just that. If she wants the world, I'll deliver it to her on a silver fucking platter. If she wants me gone and to never speak to her again, I'll leave. It would gut me to leave not only her, but also Mack and the club, but I would do it for her. I'd pack everything up and never look back. I'd spend the rest of my life regretting everything I did to hurt her and pray that one day, she'd forgive me.

And if she wants me, I'll make sure that I'm the best man I can be for her. I'll never take anything for granted, especially my time with her. I'll tell her how I feel about her, how much I love her and need her in my life, and that I want her to be my girl. *Officially.*

Now that I realize what she means to me, I'll do

everything in my power to make sure she feels loved and protected.

Mack interrupts my thoughts by coming up to me at the bar. I've been sitting here for the past hour, just staring at the wall. I have a bottle of beer in front of me, but I haven't taken one drink. I want so badly to drown out the pain with alcohol, but worry that if I do and we find her, I won't be able to do what needs to be done.

"I think you should get some sleep. We still haven't found anything, but when we do—and I promise you, we will—you're going to need your strength," he says with authority, but also compassion.

It saddens me to think back to all the years I've had with Mack and I never really appreciated any of them. He's always been there for me and I took it for all for granted. That's another thing I'm going to have to change when this is all said and done. I can only hope it's not too late.

"I don't think I could even if I wanted to," I say. Every time I close my eyes, I picture Harlow somewhere scared and alone, crying out to me. But when I try to reach out to her, it's like she's always just out of reach.

Taking a seat beside me, he opens a beer I didn't even see him grab and sets it in front of him. He doesn't take a drink, just has it sitting there as if it comforts him somehow to know it's there. Kind of like me, I guess.

"She'll be all right, ya know. Whatever hell she's going through, she'll be okay." He tries to reassure me, but it's not doing any good. The situation feels hopeless. *I* feel hopeless.

"When my dad died, I was devastated and enraged. I thought the world wronged me by allowing him to be taken away from me. I wanted the man that killed him to pay, but I wanted the whole world to pay too. But this…what's happening *right now*…it's different," I say, trying to explain to him what I'm feeling, hoping that he'll know how to fix it. You know that feeling you get when you're young and hurt, you tell your dad what's going on and he somehow magically can make it better. *That's* what I'm hoping for right now.

"Even before Harlow left two years ago, she meant the world to me. I just didn't realize it then. I mean, I knew she was a good friend and I cared immensely about her. Then while she was gone, I felt the same way I did when my father died; like I had been wronged. I was angry at the world, at myself, and at her for leaving me willingly. I hated her in a way for the longest time. But then she came back. And yeah, she was different, but it was in a raw way that I could relate to. She'd lost the only person she could count on, and I wanted to be the one to help her through it."

Finally turning to look at him, I finish. "And I think I did. I helped her through her anger and helped her heal. Like you did for me. She'll never be the same, but that's okay. I realized yesterday that I love her, Mack. I probably have from the very beginning, but it just hit me like a ton of bricks landed on my chest. And now she's gone. I don't even want to think about what she's going through. If something happens to her and I lose her, I don't think I'll survive. I never thought I'd feel anything like I felt when my dad died, but I do, except it's worse. I can't lose her, Mack."

We sit there in silence for a few moments, each digesting what I said. When he does finally speak, his voice is clogged with emotion. "I understand what you're feeling, son. I may not love a woman the way you love Harlow, Toby loves Sara, or Blaze loves Dani, but I get it. I do. And I promise you that you will never have to find out if you could survive without her because you won't have to. We *will* find her and we *will* get her back. And do you want to know how I know that?" he asks, though I'm not sure if he actually wants an answer, so I just shake my head. "I know that because after everything you both have been through, you both deserve to be happy. You both deserve a long life filled with love. So we will find her, Louie. She'll be all right."

Both of us stare at each other for a few seconds before turning back around to face the bar and our untouched beers, each in our own heads.

I love Mack for what he said, I just pray that he's right.

"Now if you won't sleep, what do ya say we head out to check in personally with Blaze and Toby? They're watching the Kings and it'll give us something to do while we wait on news about Harlow."

Nodding, I get up and head outside. Straddling my bike, I wait for Mack to pull out first before following him.

I really hope Blaze and Toby have some news for us because I feel the monster gnawing at my insides, just begging to come out. But I don't want to let him because Mack was right, I need to feel all these emotions to be any use to Harlow.

***

Twenty minutes later, Mack and I are pulling up next to Blaze and Toby's bikes. They parked about three blocks away from where they are keeping watch so no one would know we are here.

Toby and Blaze are holed up in a house right across the street for the Kings' compound. We actually paid for the owners to go on a much needed vacation, which they were all too happy to take. Turns out the Kings don't make the best neighbors. *Go figure.*

Opening the door, we make our way upstairs. Toby is sitting at a card table they must have brought in looking at something on a computer and Blaze is sitting at the window with binoculars. "Hey, brother. So what type of set-up we got going on here and do we have anything new?" I ask Blaze.

Mack takes a seat by Toby, leaning over to check out what he's doing on the computer.

"Well, nothing has been going on here, that's for sure. No one in or out in the past hour and a half. The place is dead. On the bright side to that though, I was able to sneak in the back and put a surveillance camera out there. If anything happens back there, we now have eyes on it."

Nodding, I look over to Toby. "Jax is in the process of setting up the rest of the security cameras at the other locations were we have a blind spot.

This way, nothing will get past us. The last one should be up soon." Liking what they did and where their head is on this, I relax a little. They've got my back and in turn, they have my girls back.

I guess you could say I was a little worried how they'd react to this after what went down with Sara a few years ago and how it almost tore us all apart. And even though their women aren't in danger this time, I worried how they'd feel about going no holds barred looking for Harlow. I mean, let's face it, she's probably not the most liked girl even though she has gotten better since she's been back. But she was downright rude when she first got here and I know Toby and Blaze were both itching to give her a piece of their minds.

"Good. That's good," I say.

"Have you heard back from the other brothers? Any noise or movement on their ends?" Blaze asks without even looking at us. He's still looking out the window, always watching. But he's damn good at it.

"Only person who I've heard from is Slayer. He's got his ears to the ground, but there's been nothing. Louie, why don't you make a call to Tom Tom, see if there's anything he's got for us," Mack says, then turns back toward the computer.

Standing up, I dig my phone out of my pocket and hit speed dial for Tom Tom. "Hey, brother." He answers on the second ring.

"Hey, man. We're with Blaze and Toby. They've got a nice set-up here with security cameras, so anything happens behind their line of sight, we'll still be able to see. Jax is finishing setting up the cameras at the rest of the locations." I fill him in on the comings and goings on my end before asking him, "Anything new on your end?"

"Nah, man. It's like these pieces of shit know we're watching. There is zero movement and everything is radio silent. I was even able to get in touch with one of their suppliers who owed me a favor. He tried calling them in, was going to say there was a problem with one of their shipments, but they ain't budging. Didn't even answer, man. Something is definitely going down."

I don't like the sound of that. You don't just *not* answer a call from your supplier, so what the fuck is going on? If it doesn't have anything to do with Harlow, it has something to do with us, that I know for sure. We're the only club within an hundred miles radius.

"All right, brother. Keep us posted," I say before ending the call.

"Tom Tom has nothing. Said there's no movement anywhere and they couldn't even lure them out by using one of their suppliers." I fill the guys in, maybe they'll have some insight to what the fuck is going on.

Everyone is quiet for a moment, taking in the new information and trying to come up with a good reason the Kings have gone dark.

It doesn't make sense, even if they did have Harlow. You'd think that they'd try to keep up some sort of ruse. They'd know we'd be looking and they know that we are aware of them. Sure, they don't know how closely we've been keeping an eye out, but they're the only MC close by. And they would have always been our first lead whether there was reason to suspect them or not. That's mainly why we are here now. We don't have a solid lead but they are technically a rival.

"I wish there was a way we could get a bug in inside. If we knew there was no one there, we could sneak in and plant it. Then we'd be able to have ears on the inside instead of just eyes on the outside." Blaze is the first to speak up.

I look at Mack because even though I think it's a great idea and would say we should risk it, anything to get more information on what they are up to, he's the only one that can make that call.

"Do we know if there is anyone inside?" he asks.

"No. We can't be one hundred percent sure, but by the looks of it and based on what I heard when I set up the security camera, I would bet they aren't there." Blaze answers.

Mack looks to Toby. "What do you think?" Even though Blaze is the one that has experience in surveillance, Toby would be the best person to send for the bug. He knows how to set them up because he's trained with Blaze, but also because he'd be the best guy if a problem arose once he was inside or if we are wrong and there are members within those walls. Blaze was always behind the scenes with security while Toby was front line in the Marines *and* a fighter in the cage.

Looking to Blaze, he asks, "Do we have mics? That way we can communicate. I'll be your eyes and ears on the inside and you'll be my eyes out here." See, they'd make a great team for this. I just wish there was something I could do to help with this, but it's probably best for me to stay where I am.

"Yeah, man. I've got 'em. I can have you wired in two minutes, then we can get this done," Blaze answers, then we all look to Mack for approval.

Nodding, he stands up. "Let's get this shit done."

Blaze gets to work setting everything up and Toby goes through his weapons to make sure he's well equipped in case he runs into problems. Within five minutes, everything is ready to go.

"Louie, you're on the computer. Let me know if you see anything happening on the screen. Mack, you and I are at the window. You'll keep lookout while I run interference to Toby. Everyone ready?" Blaze asks. He's damn good at this kind of shit, but I suppose he'd better be; he does it for a living. But I will say one thing; he'd make a hell of a leader. Nothing against Tom Tom because he's a great vice president, but with him getting older, it might be time to talk to Mack about him stepping down and Blaze taking his place.

"All right, let's do this, boys," Toby says before heading down the stairs and out the door.

Since I'm at the computer, I can't see him, but I know he's in good hands and he knows what he's doing.

I listen to Mack and Blaze talk back and forth and communicate with Toby, but my main focus is on the screens. I need to be sharp in case something shows up on the cameras.

Fifteen minutes later, Toby was able to plant five bugs within the clubhouse without trouble. There was no one inside so he was able to work efficiently and quickly. Now, if something happens while they are there, we'll be able to hear it.

Toby is on his way back to the house when I see a truck pull up outside of one of the warehouses the Kings have outside of town. It's their oldest one and was said to be pretty much abandoned. Word is they never go there anymore but want to keep it in case there is an emergency. We weren't even going to keep an eye on it because we wanted to put our men where we thought we'd be more likely to see something, but Mack and I didn't like it. We didn't want to take the chance of missing anything.

We didn't have enough men to place someone out there, but since Blaze thought of the idea with the security cameras, I guess now we're able to watch it. And lucky we are because someone just showed up.

"Someone just arrived at Warehouse 34," I say, but I don't take my eyes off the screen.

I can hear Toby coming up the stairs and see Blaze and Mack move toward me out of the corner of my eye. And then I see it; a man I've never seen before gets out of the driver's side door and walks over to the passenger side. He's watching his surroundings, making sure he's not being followed or watched.

"Who the fuck is that?" Blaze asks, looking at the screen.

"He must be one of the members that showed up from outta town. He's not one of them from around here, that I can tell." This is from Toby.

I keep quiet and watch. I don't like this guy, there's just something about him. The way he walks and the general vibe coming off of him in waves. He's up to something.

Opening the passenger door, he's out of view for a few moments, then when he comes back in sight, he's carrying what looks like a body.

Sitting up straighter, I lean closer, trying to get a good look at the body. Trying to see if I can make out if it's male or female. But I *know* it's her. And when he opens the door to the warehouse, the movement causes the person's head to roll a little and a mess of long hair falls over his arm.

Standing up abruptly, my chair flies behind me, falling down onto the floor.

I don't stop when Mack orders me to as I fly down the stairs or when Toby asks if I could tell who it is. It's Harlow, and we all know it. Now it's time to go get my girl and kill the fucker that took her.

It's time for the monster to come out and play.

CHAPTER 18

Harlow

I feel like I've been in and out of it for days, *weeks* even.

I start feeling myself wake up and come back into the present, but then the pain overtakes my body and I slip back into the darkness. It's better there; no pain, no fear, and no hopes of being rescued. I've thrown that hope right out the window. I don't know exactly when I realized I'm not going to be saved and that no one will find me, but I can feel it in my bones now. *I'm going to die here.*

When I slip back into consciousness this time, the pain bombards me but the darkness is elusive. It seems just beyond my reach. I want to be taken away again, go back to the numb black hole I was in, but my mind won't let me this time. It's like it wants me to suffer—to feel every bruise, every cut, everything that is broken inside me.

I'm sitting in a hard, cold chair with my arms

tied behind my back. My arms hurt from losing blood flow, my leg and head hurts like a bitch and is pounding, and my chest hurts worse than it did before. If I didn't have a broken rib before, I definitely do now.

"Rise and shine, Harlow," Titus says from a distance, but he's moving closer, that much I can tell.

Opening my eyes, I take stock of what condition my body is in. I know I hurt everywhere, but I need to see what I'm dealing with.

The first time I woke up, my ribs hurt. Then, when I went through the table, everything in my back and head hurt. It still does but I can't focus on any of those injuries. My face is throbbing from the swollen eye, but what I'm curious about is the cut I know that adorns my forehead. Blood is no longer seeping down my face so either he patched me up or it stopped bleeding. My guess would be the latter. Why patch me up if you're just going to torture and kill me?

Then there is my leg. Looking down, I notice a bloody bandage wrapped around my leg and what looks like a make-shift tourniquet. He *did* patch me up. But why? It wasn't out of the goodness of his heart, that much I know for a fact. It was probably so I wouldn't die from blood loss before he finished whatever he has planned for me.

Next, I take in my surroundings. We are no longer in the house we were at the last time I was fully awake and trying to run to save my life.

I try to take everything in to see if I recognize the place, but again, it's nowhere I've ever been before.

We are in what looks like a warehouse or storage shed. It's big and wide open. There are only a few windows and barely anything inside. There is a workbench to my right with a few tools and a box sitting on it. Other than that, there is nothing besides me and Titus.

"Where are we?" I ask, barely able to get the words out my mouth is so dry.

"We are at an impasse, if you will. You see, I've come to realize that you will not come willingly to me and no matter how much forcing you would be a thrill, you'll fight till your death. And me, well, I'm not letting you go. You're *mine*. So we are at a stalemate at this moment. I'm trying to figure out what it is I want to do with you," he says, then he's contemplative.

"I don't suppose if I told you that you either submit to me or die that you'd be more willing, would you?" he asks with an innocent smile, but he's anything *but* innocent.

I don't even have to think of what my answer would be. "I'd rather die than give myself over to you." I don't have the energy to add more contempt, but I put as much loathing and truth into my words as I can. I would rather rot in hell than be with him.

"Didn't think so." He doesn't sound angry or even disappointed in my answer. He knew what my answer was going to be before he even asked.

"What are you going to do to me?" I want to know so I can be ready. I know he's going to kill me, but is he going to do it right now or does he have other plans first? I want to delay and have hope that Louie is looking for me and will come to my rescue, but there's no use; it's not going to happen. I'm going to die today and I'm okay with it. Well, as okay as a person can be when you know you're about to be killed by a psychopath.

On the bright side, I'll be able to see my brother again. I'll be able to hear his voice, feel his arms around me, and see his smile. And even though my life hasn't been the greatest, I only have one regret; *Louie*. I regret leaving and not telling him goodbye. I regret not coming back to him sooner. I regret how much time we wasted. And I regret not telling him how much he means to me.

It's messed up that people don't realize their true feelings until it's too late. I wish I could go back to the last time I saw him and stop him from leaving. I wish I would have told him right away about the flowers so he would have known what was going on. I would've told him about the flowers, the letter, the phone calls, and the feeling of being watched. But mostly, I'd tell him that I love him.

"Well, sunshine, I haven't decided what I'm going to do with you yet. You see, I want you for myself, but since you seem to fight me at every turn, that makes it difficult. I suppose I could force it on you until you fight to your death for your freedom. *Or*, I could just kill you now. Which would you prefer?"

I can't believe he's rationally talking like this. Asking me if I want him to kill me. But it's better than any alternative he's given me.

"Just kill me now," I say, ready for it. I've made as much peace as I can and now I just want it to be over with. I don't want the pain I feel within every molecule of my body. I don't want to look at Titus and see his disgusting face, knowing he took me from my family. I just want to get on with it.

Stepping closer so he's right in front of me, he takes out a knife. Thinking he's going to follow through, I close my eyes and wait for death. But it never comes.

"That would be too easy, though. I think I'll keep you around a little longer and see if I can break you," he says before slamming his knife deep into the leg that wasn't damaged from the tempered glass.

"AAAHHHH!" I scream. I feel every inch of the serrated edge of the knife rip through my skin and muscle. It's lodged so deep that I think he hit bone.

Instead of removing the knife, he leaves it in, but does remove his hand so there isn't so much pressure on it.

Taking shuddering breaths, I try to think of anything but the pain. If I can get my mind around it, maybe I'll be able to last longer. He intends to torture me, that much is certain, but I don't want to pass out again; from either pain or blood loss. I need to be coherent through this or else I have no idea what he'll do. He hasn't taken advantage the other times I've been knocked out, but who's to say he wouldn't now that he knows this is doomed. That I'd rather die than be with him.

No, I need to stay awake.

"Change your mind, sunshine? Want to make a different choice?" he asks in a sweet voice. His promise is to take away the pain I feel physically from his abuse, but it won't make things better. If anything, it would make it worse. I'd rather defy him at every turn and feel the pain of a thousand deaths than let him win.

"*No*," I spit.

"Hm, that's too bad. It'd be fun to ruffle your feathers in a different way, but I'll just have to settle for this instead," he says, then his hand goes back to the knife and twists it in my leg before he pulls it out.

A bloodcurdling scream tears past my lips before I can clamp them shut. I don't want to give him the satisfaction of hearing me scream. And I won't beg for my life. I'll endure it all and just before death takes me, I'll laugh in his face.

Titus wipes the blade off on his jeans, then makes his way to the box I saw sitting on the work bench. He takes out a bottle of alcohol, a large gauze pad, and tape before making his way back toward me.

Unscrewing the lid off the alcohol, he doesn't give me any time to think before he dumps it over my leg where his knife was moments ago. It feels like he dumped acid in my wound, it burns so bad but I'm able to hold my scream in this time, though I can feel myself getting dizzy from the pain.

Taking the gauze, he folds it and places it over the bleeding wound roughly, then he wraps the tape all the way around my leg.

"Why are you doing this?" I ask. I'm not meaning the torture, I mean why is he hurting me and then bandaging me up?

"Because I'm not done with you yet," he says. His harsh tone is back. Good. I'd rather him be this way than use that sickly sweet voice. He sounded more like a maniac when he was sounding nice while hurting me.

After putting that first aid stuff back into the box, he comes back with a pair of pliers. I wonder briefly about what he's going to do to me with those, but it doesn't really matter. It's going to hurt and it's going to be nasty, whatever it is he plans to do.

Undoing the rope that secured my hands behind me, they fall limply to my sides. Pain shoots up my arms from all the blood rushing back into my hands, but I don't cry out.

"There's really no sense in keeping you tied up anymore. Not like you could make it far if you managed to get away anyway." He chuckles as if it's the funniest thing on earth to him. *Bastard.*

"Now. Let's see if we can make you scream. Make you beg for it to stop."

Taking hold of my right hand, he positions the pliers around the middle knuckle of my pinky finger. Squeezing the pliers, I feel slight pressure before he pulls harshly out and then to the side, effectively breaking my finger.

I'm unable to hold in my scream. I don't think there was any way I could with the amount of pain I feel in my finger. It's almost worse than the knife.

"Ah, there's that beautiful sound," he says as he releases my finger, only to position it around my ring finger now. "Let's see if we can continue the beautiful melody of your dying song."

Taking a gasping breath, I wait for the pain of the next finger to be broken.

Clamping the pliers down on the finger, he pulls

it out to the point the pressure starts to turn into pain, but he just holds it there. He's *playing* with me. Then, when I'm not ready for it, he twists and I hear the pop and crunch of the bones breaking.

"Ah! *Please*! Please, just stop!" I cry. I'm angry at myself for begging but I can't take any more pain. I just can't.

"Stop? Sunshine, I can't. You owe your screams of pain to me for denying me what's mine. Your torment is only beginning," he says before ripping the pliers from my ring finger and instantly taking my middle finger and almost tearing it right off my hand.

And I reach my limit. The dizziness and nausea takes hold and bile empties from my stomach, landing all over me. Some even makes it onto Titus. *Good.*

I feel a little better after my stomach empties. It's like I was able to vomit all the pain and misery out of my body. But making a mess all over Titus has his face turning red and his eyes practically bulging out of his face. If I would have known a little vomit would have pushed him over the edge, I would have done it a long time ago.

"You nasty fucking cunt!" he roars, then makes a fist before punching me in the face. Blood pours out of my nose and drips down my chin.

Then, he drives his fist into my stomach, causing me to curl in on myself and fall off the chair.

This is it. This is where he ends my life. No more torturing me or making me scream. He's too far gone now. He's done with me and will finally put an end to all of it. Then I can be at peace. I won't feel the pain any longer.

Titus kicks me in the side, then reaches down to haul me to my knees by my hair. Reaching behind him, he pulls a hand gun out and points it at my head. "Say goodbye, bitch," he snarls, spit flying out of his mouth and hitting my face.

Before Titus is able to pull the trigger, the door to the warehouse busts open. And there, standing there with fire shooting out of eyes like the devil himself, is Louie.

CHAPTER 19

Louie

Kicking in the door, the first thing I see is Harlow broken and bloody, kneeling on the ground with the fucker standing above her. And he's got a gun pointed to her head.

I feel myself vibrate with a level of rage I've never felt before. I want to skin this motherfucker alive, pour acid on his exposed flesh, then watch him burn while he screams and begs for death. I've never felt this level of anger before. It's so much different from when my father was murdered. I feel empowered, invincible, and almighty. I can feel power rage through my veins just begging to be released on this guy. It's almost scary the way I feel.

But what scares me the most is the almost peaceful look on Harlow's face. I can see the pain she must be feeling, but she also looks ready to die—ready to give up and leave me. But I won't let her. Not this time.

I hate myself for putting her in this position. After all, it's because of me and the club she's here. He took her to get to us, to make the Sinners pay. I don't know why or what they have planned, but I won't let him take club business out on Harlow.

The man holding her by the hair turns around to face me, a sneer taking over his face. "Well, well, well. I was wondering if you were gonna show up and try to save the day," the guy says.

Taking a step forward, I keep my hands balled into fists at my side. I don't need him getting jumpy and pulling the trigger on Harlow. If he does, she's dead.

"Let her go," I growl, needing to get him away from her. I want to kill this fucker, but I want to do it with my bare hands. I want to make him feel the amount of pain he made Harlow endure.

"Now why would I do that?" he asks as if he's confused about the situation.

"Your beef is with me and my club, *not* with her. So just let her go and deal with me," I say, praying that he has one bone in his body that is prideful. If he is a respectable member of the MC, he'll handle this confrontation with me, and not a woman.

He laughs, but he does lower his gun. "On the contrary, I have no beef with your club. Well, besides the fact that you took something that belongs to me. Put your hands all over it. Stuck your *dick* into it." His sneer is back, but I'm thoroughly confused. What the fuck does he mean we *took something of his*? Unless...

"She was supposed to by *mine*, not yours! And if I can't have her, *no one* will!" He turns around at

226

the same time, bringing the gun back up to Harlow's head, but I'm quicker.

Reaching behind me, I pull my gun out from behind my back and shoot him in the shoulder, which causes him to drop the gun and grunt in pain.

I move quickly toward Harlow, but he recovers faster than I thought he would. Wrapping his arm around her neck in a chokehold, he stands behind her, blocking any chance I had to take another shot at him. I can't get to him without going through her.

Halting my advance, I keep my gun aimed but don't intend to fire unless I get a clear shot and Harlow is out of harm's way. I won't risk hitting her with my bullet.

Shifting my focus to her for a second, I notice that she's gone ghostly pale and she looks to be on the cusp of passing out. Blood gushes out of her head from a cut on her forehead and out of her nose. She seems to be having trouble breathing and both legs are bleeding from an unknown trauma. She's not going to last much longer. I need to hurry the fuck up and get this over with so I can get her to a hospital. She can't die on me.

"Now I can see you noticing she's in bad shape. If I had to guess, she only has a few minutes longer before the blood loss is too much and she passes out. But the question is; will she wake up again?" he speaks behind her, pulling her back toward a workbench.

Grabbing a gasoline can, he dumps a little on her which makes her scream out as it mixes into her wounds, then starts dumping it on the ground as he makes his way toward a back door.

"Now since we're in this little standoff, I'll give you two choices. I can tell you want to kill me for what I've done to little sunshine here, but you also want to save her. So you can either come after me and exact your revenge or you can be her hero. But choose fast," he says before shoving her to the ground a few feet where he's standing, while striking a match and throwing it down on the ground.

As soon as the match was thrown, he takes off out the door, too quick for me to take a shot.

Flames start to take root and spread toward Harlow lying limply on the floor. With no time to go after him, I sprint to Harlow. There was never really a choice of who I would go after. The monster may have taken over my body, but I'm not about to let Harlow burn just so I can kill that fucker. There will be time for that later; after I get her out of here and out of immediate danger.

"*Harlow*! Wake up, babe," I yell as I crouch down beside her. She's not moving and her eyes are closed. I don't know if she's dead or just passed out, but with the flames making their way closer to us, I don't have time to check. I can only pray that she's just passed out from the blood loss and the pain of her injuries.

Picking her up, I head toward the same door her tormentor fled out of, but it won't open. He must have locked it before he fled.

By now the fire has spread throughout the building, all the way up to the ceiling. We're running out of time to get out of here. If we don't make it out fast, we'll *both* burn to death.

Running carefully with her in my arms, I try not to jar her, but my first step causes her eyes to fly open and a scream tears past her lips.

"I'm sorry, babe. But we have to get out of here quick." I continue running but as we make it to the middle of the warehouse, the smoke is so thick she starts coughing, which causes her to cry out in pain.

"We're almost there. Stay with me. I've got you." I try to comfort her, but I don't even think she's hearing me, the pain too much for her to concentrate on anything else.

I'm a few feet from the door when shots start to ring out outside the warehouse. My brothers must be here and are gunning that motherfucker down. I'm pissed because I wanted to be the one to kill him, but I'm thankful my brothers are here to help. As long as that sonofabitch is dead, that's all that really matters, I guess.

Almost to the door, I hear a big bang and the ground shakes, knocking me off balance. I start to fall with Harlow in my arms, and the building starts to fall down around us.

Landing on my side as to not crush her, I try to get back up again to make it out when something big and heavy falls down on my legs.

"*Fuck!*" I roar, pain shooting up my legs. Trying to move, I realize that I'm pinned.

Looking over to Harlow, I see her open her eyes and take in the scene around us.

"Harlow! You need to get out of here. The place is falling apart. You need to go!" I yell, trying to get her to save herself. Once I know she's safe, I'll be able to focus solely on freeing myself.

She looks at me with fear in her eyes, but it's not for herself. "No. I'm not leaving you!" she says with pain in her voice, though I think it's more from her injuries than thinking I won't make it.

"I'll be fine. I promise, but you have to get yourself to safety. I'll be right behind you," I tell her, though I'm starting to doubt that, but I'll say anything to get her to leave me so she's safe. I *need* her to be safe.

Harlow starts to get up onto her elbows and I think she's going to listen and crawl out of here and leave me behind, but she doesn't. She army crawls toward me. "Harlow! Go! Leave me!"

I frantically try to unpin myself. I need to get her out of here. She's not listening to me.

"No! I can't leave you, Louie. I love you. I won't leave you," she cries and I know we are both doomed. I can't get free and she won't listen to me. She won't leave me behind, even to save herself.

I reach out my hand, determined to touch her one last time before it's over for us. "I love you, Harlow," I tell her, hoping she can hear more than just the words, but know what she means to me.

"I love you too," she says around her coughing from the smoke, then her eyes close and I fear she's dead.

"Harlow! Open your eyes, babe!" I yell, not ready to let her leave me yet.

Just then, the door a few feet from us opens and I see Toby and Blaze rush in, searching the area for us.

"Over here," I yell, starting to cough from the smoke too.

Finally finding us, they run to us; Blaze immediately starting to move the debris off my legs and Toby going to Harlow's side.

"Is she okay?" I ask, but he doesn't answer me. "*Tell me, dammit*! Is she alive?" I demand again.

This time, he looks up at me with sadness in her eyes. "No!" I scream, fighting with Blaze to get free so I can get closer to her.

"She's alive, brother. But barely. I need to get her out of here and get her to the hospital," he says in a rush, then he picks her up and runs out of the building.

Blaze continues to work on me while I just lay there, watching the door where Toby disappeared with my girl.

"She'll be all right, man. You have to believe that. But you need to help me. The building is still coming down and if we don't get you out of here soon, we'll both be a pile of charred bones," Blaze says, his words snapping me out of my grief.

Seconds later, I'm finally free. I try to stand up on my own, with a little help from my brother, but I fall right back down.

"Put your arm around me," Blaze yells over the noise of the building falling down around us.

He crouches down so I'm able to wrap my arm around his shoulders and he starts to drag me out of the building.

Once outside, I take in deep gulps of fresh air but end up choking on it. "Easy, brother," Blaze says as we make our way to a van parked a few feet away, not even sparing a second glance at the burning building behind us.

I don't see Toby with Harlow or even Mack and Jax. "Where is everyone? Did they take her to the hospital?" I ask, but one look at Blaze's face and I know I'm missing something. "What am I missing?" I demand, needing to know what's going on.

"Let's get you to the hospital, man. We need to get you checked out and we have to see how Harlow and Mack are doing," he says as he helps me into the front seat of the van, then slams the door before making his way around to the driver's side.

When he's inside and peeling out, I ask, "What do you mean see how Harlow and Mack are doing? What the fucked happened to Mack?" I ask, getting more frustrated without having any answers to what happened. *Mack is in the hospital?* Why?

"He was shot, Louie."

I don't know what to say to that. I heard shots ring out when I was trying to get Harlow out, but I assumed it was them shooting the fucker that escaped out of the warehouse after leaving me and Harlow to burn. But now he's telling me Mack was the one shot?

"What the fuck happened?" I yell, needing to know exactly what transpired outside.

"When we got to the warehouse, you were already inside. We figured you'd be able to get Harlow out and take care of any problems, but we surrounded the building in case he tried getting away while you were saving Harlow," he explains as he speeds down the road toward the hospital.

"He came out the back door and when we didn't

see you behind him, we knew we had to take care of him for you. But he spotted us right away and started shooting at us. We were able to take cover, but Mack was hit. It's bad, Louie. He was hit in the back as he was dodging behind a dumpster. He lost a lot of blood and wasn't conscious when Jax was able to get him out of here while Toby and I took care of the sonofabitch that started all of this."

I assume by *taking care of him*, he means they killed him, but I need confirmation. I have to know he's dead and paid for his sins.

"Did you kill him?" I ask in a hard voice. I almost hope that they didn't so I can hunt him down and kill him myself, but I know they wouldn't have let him get away. They would have done anything necessary to end him.

"Yeah, he's dead. Toby was able to get a headshot on the motherfucker," he says with contempt, angry that he didn't get to kill the fucker himself. *Get in line*. I'm pissed about that too.

Minutes later, we're screeching to a stop outside the emergency doors of the local hospital. I don't like that we aren't in our town—I feel too exposed and vulnerable—but going off of what Blaze said about Mack's condition and seeing firsthand the condition Harlow is in, I understand the urgency to just get them to the closest hospital. Doesn't mean we won't have them moved the first chance we get.

Rushing inside with the help of Blaze, we find all of our brothers huddled together in the waiting room.

"What's going on? Where are they?" I ask, needing to know where they are and if we've heard anything yet.

"They took Mack in for surgery. The bullet grazed his spine. They won't know what the outcome will be until they can stabilize him," Tom Tom says first.

When no one says anything about Harlow, I start to get pissed. "And Harlow," I seethe. Somebody better fill me in real quick or else I'm going to start dropping bodies and tearing this place apart looking for her.

"She's in surgery too. She has so many injuries they weren't able to update us before they took her away. The only thing we can do is wait." Jax's words don't give me any comfort.

Needing to know more, I release Blaze and try to make my way toward the nurse's station, but my legs give out. *Fuck*! I forgot about my own injuries. But those are just going to have to wait. I need to know what's going on with my girl.

"Whoa, brother. We need to get you into a room to have you looked at," Blaze says, trying to wrap my arm back around his shoulders, but I'm not having it.

"No! I need to find out about Harlow. They have to have more information than what they told you." Trying once more to walk, Blaze releases my arm, but moves in front of me.

"Look, I know what you must be feeling. You forget, I've been here before. *More than once*. But you aren't going to be any help to her like this. You need to take care of yourself first and let the doctors do their jobs. We should know more soon, and if not, I *promise* I will find a doctor that will tell us more." I hate that he's right. I don't want to worry about myself and get checked out, but it's the only option right now.

"Fine. I'll give them ten minutes, but if we still don't have anything, I'll find out my own way."

Knowing that's as good as he's gonna get from me, Blaze nods his head, then helps me over to a gurney in the hallway.

"I'll go find you a doctor. Don't you fucking move, or you'll deal with me." It's a half threat, but I know he'll follow through.

It won't be easy, but I'll stay put. For now. They just better hope a doctor finds us soon with news about Harlow and Mack.

CHAPTER 20

Harlow

Movement to my side brings me back from the numb darkness but I don't want to open my eyes. I don't want to see Titus beside me and wonder what new torture he'll put me through.

I think I remember Louie showing up to save me, but that was probably my mind's way of protecting me from the hell of Titus's torment.

Someone grabs my hand. I try to pull out of their grasp, but it's no use. I'm too weak and broken to get away.

My heart starts to beat faster and my breath comes in short, hard pants. He's going to hurt me again. He's going to kill me. I can't go through this anymore. I can't take any more pain.

"Harlow. It's okay, calm down. It's me, babe," I hear, but it doesn't register in my mind. I can see Titus in my mind's eye and feel the gun pressed to my head. Every injury he inflicted on me starts to pound and pain shoots through my whole body.

"No! Don't touch me!" I yell, still trying to get away from him, but my efforts are useless.

"Harlow. It's Louie. Open your eyes, babe," the voice says frantically, but it's Titus's voice I hear.

My heart is beating so fast, it feels like it's going to pound right out of my chest. I know I need to calm down, but I can't. The only thing I can think about is what Titus is going to do to me next.

"What's going on in here?" I hear a different voice say, but I can't focus on them.

"I don't know. She won't open her eyes but she's freaking out. What's wrong with her?"

I feel another set of hands on me, and I cry out, thinking it's a painful touch. "No!" I scream and start to thrash, but I'm being held down. "Let me go!"

One set of hands leaves me only to be replaced by another set. Then, I feel warmth spread through my body and everything starts to go black. But I'm happy to go. I'll do anything to get away from my tormentor.

***

I hear voices when I wake up again, but this time I recognize them as Dani and Sara. I don't know who they're talking to, but I'm just glad that they're here and not hurt by Titus.

Opening my eyes, I take in the room. I was worried that when I woke up, I'd still be in the warehouse, but I'm in a hospital.

I see movement out of the corner of my eyes so I lay real still and hold my breath. *It's Titus*, I know it is. I don't want to draw attention to myself. But then I remember Dani and Sara. I need to get them out of here so he can't hurt them.

Taking a deep breath, I open my mouth a scream. "Dani! Sara! Get out of here before he gets you!" My heart rate has started to pick up again but I don't care if I have a heart attack. I just need to know that they'll be safe from Titus.

Titus jumps up from his sitting position beside me and reaches out to me. He grabs a hold of my shoulders, but I try to fight him off. I feel the pain in my chest, legs, and fingers rip through me, but I don't care. I won't let him take Dani and Sara.

"Get out of here!" I yell again, hoping this time they'll listen.

"Harlow! Harlow, stop fighting. It's Louie!" Titus says. This must be a new form of punishment for not going with him, but I won't fall for his tricks. It's not Louie, it's Titus.

"No!" I try to fight harder, but the pain is beginning to be too much. I start to shake all over and cry in devastation. I'm never going to get away from him.

"Nurse!" he yells and when a woman in blue scrubs rushes toward me, I start fighting harder again. He must have paid someone to drug me as a new way of hurting me.

"Stay away from me!" I scream at her, but she continues forward.

Seeing Dani and Sara crying behind her, I think for a moment that Titus has already hurt them, but I don't see any injuries.

"*Help me!* Please!" I beg them, even though I

tried to get them to flee a few moments ago, but I can't take this anymore.

They start to cry harder and turn their heads away from me, like they can't bear to watch what is about to happen. I lose it. I'm officially alone, no one to help me, but I won't go out without a fight.

Swinging one of my arms out, I'm able to hit the nurse in the face with my hand, knocking her back a step. "Harlow, stop!" Titus yells, but I won't stop. I'm going to keep defying him, keep fighting him until my last breath.

Titus pins my arms to the bed and the nurse comes toward me again. I can see blood leaking out of her lip but that's all the damage I was able to inflict on her. Then I feel the pinch of the needle into my neck and everything goes hazy again. I'm back into the darkness. I'm back to my safe haven.

***

Louie

As soon as I feel Harlow go limp under my arms, I release her.

Looking to the girls first, I see they're both crying and holding onto each other.

Then I look to the nurse. She seems to be only a little frazzled and her lip is split a little, but other than that, she looks to be all right.

"I'm so sorry," I say, hoping she doesn't try to press charges on Harlow. She's not in her right frame of mind. Everything that happened to her was too much and now her mind is the one tormenting her.

"Don't worry about me. I'm all right," she says as she disposes of the syringe that was able to calm Harlow down.

"What's the matter with her?" Sara chokes out around her tears. They're still holding onto each other, but they've moved closer.

"She has PTSD. Due to the nature of her injuries, I suspect she went through quite a lot of trauma. Something must have triggered the episode and she was transported back to what happened to her," the nurse explains.

My bum leg finally gives out and I fall into the chair hard. That fucker is dead and he's still tormenting her.

"Will she be okay?" Dani asks, though I'm not sure I want to hear the answer. What if she never gets past this? What if she's having more than just a panic attack, but actually a psychotic breakdown? She may not be able to come back from this.

"It's going to take time and probably a lot of therapy, but she'll get better. Once we know more of what her triggers are, we'll be able to help her better." The nurse's answer isn't as bad as I thought it would be. Maybe we can help her get through this after all.

"What can we do to help?" I ask, finally feeling some hope again. I thought she was out of the woods after she was out of surgery and they were able to repair most of the damage done to her. She still has a long way to go with recovery, but I thought it would just be the *physical* stuff she'd have to get over. Not *mental*.

"Well, there are lots of things you can do to help with her recovery. First and foremost, just be patient with her. It's going to take time for her to get better mentally, but she'll get there. Also, it wouldn't be a bad idea to research PTSD. The more you know about it, the more you'll be able to help her," she says as she takes a seat on the other side of the bed. Dani and Sara move forward and take a seat by me.

"We can do that. What else?" Dani asks.

"Don't pressure her into talking. It's important that you be there for her and listen to her when she's ready to talk about something, but don't push her. It'll only make things worse. Also, make sure that you don't take things personally. Sometimes it will be difficult but you can't let it affect you. You need to understand that sometimes people with PTSD don't have control over their behavior. There's no magic switch she can just flip on and off, but with time and treatment, they will get better. It's a gradual process, but she will get better."

The door opens and Toby and Blaze walk in. Sensing the mood in the room, they each stand behind their girl and are silent.

The nurse continues on. "Also, people with PTSD will see the world differently. It'll seem like a dangerous and frightening place at times, just like what happened a few moments ago. She was frightened and reacted. You'll need to understand this because if you aren't careful, it could damage the ability she has to trust you or herself around you. Anything you can do to rebuild her sense of security will contribute immensely to her recovery."

"How do we do that?" Blaze asks. I almost

forgot he was here, I was so caught up in my own head, trying to think of ways I can help Harlow get through this.

"Well, there are a few things you can do. Express your commitment to her, whether it's a friendship role or a lover's role. Let her know you aren't going anywhere. Don't be spontaneous; having structured routines and predictable schedules will enhance her feelings of security. It will help her feel safe around you. Minimizing stress will help too."

Fuck, I feel like I need to be taking notes. How the hell am I'm going to be able to do all of this?

Dani, noticing my unease, reaches out and places her hand on my knee. "It's okay, Louie. We'll all help her. She'll be fine," she reassures me.

"Yes, you all can help. In fact, I encourage that. The more people who surround her and support her will help the healing process. I know it seems like a lot right now, but the main thing is just be there for her. Let her know you believe in her and that everything will be okay. Tell her how strong she is and brave. She'll get through this and so will all of you." The nurse stands up to leave.

"I'll be back soon. I'll print some things off for you all as well, and like I said, educate yourself. The more you know, the easier it will be to help her." The nurse leaves the room.

We're all quiet for a while, each thinking about what the nurse told us. I feel overwhelmed with all the information, but I'm determined to help Harlow through this. I'll be strong for her and make sure she knows that she's safe with me. With all of us.

***

Later that night, Harlow is still sleeping and it's just Dani and me. I haven't left the room, only getting up to go to the bathroom and even then, I don't have to leave the room for that.

"How's the leg?" she asks, concern lacing her voice.

"Hurts like hell, but I'll be all right. Could've been worse."

I ended up with a hairline fracture in my fibula from the warehouse falling down on me. They were worried that I wouldn't stay off of it like I should and end up breaking it all the way, so they put me in a cast. *Fuckers*.

"Yeah, it could've," she says, then she's quiet for a while.

"Have you been up to see Mack lately?" I ask. I feel like shit not going up to see him in the ICU, but I can't bring myself to leave Harlow.

"I saw him before I came down here. He's still asleep, but the doctors think he'll wake up soon," she says, sounding tired. I'm sure all of this is a lot for her right now. Mack being hurt, Harlow being hurt, and her trying to be here for everyone. Plus, still being there for the twins.

"How are you holding up?" I ask. Dani is like a sister to me and even though I can barely keep myself from falling apart, I need to make sure Dani's okay too.

"To be honest, I don't know. Harlow has a long way to go to recover, both physically with her leg and fingers, and mentally with the PTSD. And

Mack…we don't even know the full extent of his injuries yet. I mean, the doctor said that they were able to get the bullet out, but it grazed his spine, Louie. They have no idea if he'll be able to walk again."

When Blaze came in earlier after Mack was out of surgery, he told me that. We're all devastated but Mack is a fighter. I know he'll be able to make it out of this and still be able to walk. Nothing can keep him down for long.

"He'll be fine, Dani. Mack is the toughest sonofabitch I know, and stubborn too. Almost as stubborn as you," I say, only partly joking, but it gets the reaction I was looking for.

Dani laughs, then leans her head down on my shoulder. "I hope you're right."

"Of course I'm right, honey. I'm *always* right."

***

Harlow

Opening my eyes, I feel groggy. I hate feeling like this. It's like I'm drunk and high at the same time. And yes, I know what both of those feel like.

Turning my head slightly, I see Dani and Louie sitting beside each other sleeping, Dani's head lying on Louie's shoulder and Louie's head lying on Dani's head. The sight makes me smile.

Sighing, I straighten my head and stare up at the ceiling, thinking about the chain of events that brought me here; my brother's suicide, me not coping with the loss, coming back here, being with

Louie, Titus taking me, and finally Louie saving me.

The past few days have been a whirlwind of emotions and painful memories. I remember everything Titus did to me and I remember the hopelessness I felt thinking I wouldn't survive. And then waking up in the hospital, freaking out thinking Titus was here to finish what he started. I know I scared everyone with my outburst; not once, but twice. I can't even explain what came over me. I know Titus has to be dead. There's no way the club would let him live after everything that happened. So I knew I was safe—that I *am* safe—but my brain wouldn't listen. It just kept screaming at me to run, to fight.

I don't even know the list of my injuries but I can still feel them all. I have at least three broken fingers, broken ribs, bruised insides, and massive gashes on my legs and head. Now, I can add mental status to that long list. It's going to take me a long time to get better, but I want to get better. Not just for me, but for my family. I know they all must have been scared shitless and freaking out over my behavior. I don't want them to have to worry about me. I just want to get better and move on from this.

Movement catches me attention and I turn my head to see which one of the two is waking up. Louie stirs and seems to try to get comfortable, but then gives up on that hope. Opening his eyes, he doesn't notice I'm awake yet.

"Louie," I whisper, not wanting to wake Dani up but not being able to stay quiet either.

Whipping his head toward me, as soon as his

eyes land on mine, he's jumping up to rush toward me, but he ends up limping. Looking closer, I see him in a cast. What the hell happened to him?

"Harlow! Are you okay?' he rushes out, not seeming to care that his outburst woke Dani up.

"I'm fine, Louie. But are *you* okay? What happened to your leg?" I ask, worried about him.

Waving my question off, he takes my hand. "It's nothing, babe. Just a sprain," he says, but I know he's not telling me the truth. They don't put a full cast on you for a sprain, but I don't push him.

Smiling, I just stare into his eyes. He saved my life. I'm just so glad that he's all right and here with me.

Clearing my throat that is clogged with emotion, I say, "I'm gonna be just fine." And I know I will be. With everyone I care about by my side, and time, I'll be perfect. I'll make sure of it.

***

Louie

Dani insisted that she stay with Harlow and I make my way up to the ICU while Harlow was sleeping. I was torn between what I should do; I didn't want to leave Harlow, fearing that she'd have a breakdown again and I wouldn't be there, and needing to see Mack. I know he's still unconscious and he needs that time to heal, but I need to see him for myself to know he's okay.

Opening the door quietly, I see Blaze sitting beside Mack. "Hey, brother. How is he doing?" I ask, walking further into the room.

"No change yet. He's still sleeping. The doctors keep saying that he'll wake up soon, but he's not," Blaze says with worry evident in his voice.

Taking a seat on the other side of the bed, I look at Mack as I talk. "He'll be fine. He's just resting, building up his strength. He'll wake up when he's ready," I say, trying to sound confident. Though I try to believe what I just said, a part me has some doubt. Mack isn't old by any means, but what if the trauma was just too much for him? Or what's more, what if he wakes up and he's paralyzed? How will he get over that?

"Yeah, man. You're probably right," Blaze replies, interrupting my negative thoughts.

A few minutes later, Blaze stands up. "You good here with him for a little while? I want to go check in on Dani and call Sara to check on the kids."

Nodding, I wave him off. "Yeah, brother. Do what you need to do. I'll sit with him."

After closing the door behind him, I sit here quietly just looking at Mack. I wish he'd wake up already. I know I told Blaze we had to be patient, just like we have to be patient with Harlow, but that was me talking crap. What I really want is for him to open his eyes and tell me to grow a pair and quit acting like a bitch. Yeah, that's what I need.

When the silence is finally too much for me, I lean forward and take his hand. "Hey, Mack," I start, feeling stupid at first for talking to someone who isn't even awake, but decide to continue on. "Harlow's gonna be all right. You were right, she's strong. Though she has a long road ahead of her and there was more damage than we thought, she's a fighter. And I know with everyone supporting her, she'll be fine."

As I think about what else I want to say, I resituate my leg. It's starting to pound, but I don't want to take pain meds. I don't want to get loopy.

"I got caught in a burning building again," I say, then chuckle. "I know, it's my thing, right? At least this time I wasn't knocked out, though maybe that would have been better. Then I wouldn't have the images of Harlow bleeding all over and thinking she was dead constantly bombarding me." I still can't get that scene out of my head and I doubt I will for a long time.

"And then I find out that you were shot. Scared the shit outta me. Brought back all the memories of the last time I was in a burning building and I woke up to finding out Lyle was dead." Lyle was a close friend of mine, not just a brother. I still miss him to this day. I know he's looking down on us all though and laughing at me. Probably telling me to quit being a pussy. *Asshole*.

Sighing, I drop my head. "I've got a lot of makin' up to do. Not just with Harlow, but with you. I realized yesterday that I've been really shitty these past few years. To be honest, probably since the beginning. I thought with my dad gone that place in my heart would always be void and the pain would always be there. But that's not necessarily true. I miss my dad like crazy, but through that pain and loss, I found you. Or rather, *you* found *me*. And I know I don't say it a lot, but I want you to know how grateful I am for everything you've done for me. The kindness you've shown me. But most of all, for filling that void. I love you, old man."

"Love you too, son," Mack says in a scratchy voice.

Jerking my head up, I see that he's awake. Barely, but he's awake.

"Now quit acting like a bitch and get me some water, would ya?"

EPILOGUE

Harlow

Today I get released from the hospital. It's been a long two weeks with lots of physical therapy for my leg and talking to therapists for my PTSD, but I'm more than ready to go home. I'm not one hundred percent yet, but I'll get there.

Louie is signing my release papers and then he'll be bringing a wheelchair for me. I still have some trouble walking on the leg Titus drove his knife into because I have some nerve damage, but I don't think I need a wheelchair. Louie, on the other hand, wants me to take it easy as much as possible. Plus, since we're going to up see Mack before we leave the hospital, it might not be a bad idea.

A few minutes later, Louie comes walking into the room. "Ready, babe?" he asks with a huge smile on his face. Yeah, he's happy I get to come home too.

"Yeah. More than ready," I say, standing up from the bed to walk to where he's standing, but he rushes toward me, halting my progress.

"Whoa, Harlow. You can't be doing shit like that. I got the wheelchair for a reason, babe."

Ugh, this is going to get old real fast.

"Louie, I love you dearly, but if you don't back the fuck off I'd fear for your life," I say. I appreciate everything he's trying to do, but I need time to heal and exercise, not to be babied.

"I'm sorry. I just worry you're going to overdo it," he says sheepishly.

Pushing up onto my toes, I kiss his lips. "I know. And I love you for it, but I'm fine. Promise." I kiss him once more, then take a seat in the wheelchair to make him happy. "Now take me to see Mack, slave."

Laughing, he takes a bow. "Yes, ma'am!"

Five minutes later, we arrive at Mack's room, but before we're able to make it inside, a woman giggling stops us.

Looking silently up to Louie, I smile. I wonder who that could be.

"Knock knock," I say before I take the reins on the wheelchair and head inside. Nurse Rose is beside Mack's bed, pretending to check his vitals, but I know better. I just wish she'd stop pushing him away when he gets too close.

"Hey, you!" I say before standing up and walking over to him to give him a kiss on the cheek.

"Harlow!" Louie chastises me, but I ignore him. He's going to have to get used to it.

"I hear you're getting released for good behavior today," Mack says, smiling warmly at me.

"You heard right! I can't wait to get home and

take a nice hot shower and eat some real food. No offense," I say the last part to Nurse Rose.

"None taken, honey." She laughs, then the smile falls from her face and she turns to Mack. "All right, Mr. DeVin, make sure you do those exercises the physical therapist gave you."

"Will you spank me if I'm a naughty boy and don't follow the rules?" Mack teases, but it has no effect on her.

"No. I'll send Nurse Helga in here to punish you for not following the rules," she says, then turns to leave, but not before winking at me. Yeah, there's something going on between them. She's the perfect match for him too.

Turning back to Mack, I see him pouting, watching her leave. "Come on, Mack. Put the lip away." I pat his hand. "And you better do as she says, otherwise you'll have to deal with more than just Nurse Helga," I threaten, though nothing is worse than Nurse Helga. She's eighty years old and meaner than a hornet. I would know, she's been my nurse a few times.

"Okay! Enough with the threats. I'll do the damn exercises. Not like it's gonna change anything, though." He adds the last part softer, like he didn't want me to hear.

Mack got shot in the back and the bullet nicked his spine. They did surgery to remove it and repair any damage, but some of the nerves were hit. They think that with enough physical therapy he'll be able to walk again, but so far, he still doesn't have feeling in his legs. And hearing him doubt that he'll walk again makes me want to cry. Seeing him so down and unable to do what he loves is hard. I wish there were something I could do or say to make this better for him or fix him.

"Enough with the depressing crap. You two get outta here. I'm sure you have more pressing things to do besides sit here with an old cripple all day," Mack says, giving Louie a meaningful look. I have no idea why or what it means.

I open my mouth to argue, but the look I get from Mack warns me not to. He's more irritable lately, but I don't blame him. But I will be having a talk with him soon about his attitude toward himself and about getting better.

"We'll see you soon, okay?" I give him one more kiss, then sit back down in the wheelchair to wait for Louie to say his goodbye.

***

Louie

I hate seeing him like this, but I know he'll be all right. He's tough and he's stubborn. He won't let this keep him down for long.

"Oh, and Louie? Tell Blaze to give me a call. I want to check in and see what's been going on with the Kings," Mack tells me before we leave the room.

"Yeah, will do," I say.

Blaze is acting President while Mack is out of commission. Mack was the one who voted him in, but everyone was happy with the decision. Blaze is perfect for the job, though we all hope Mack gets back on his feet soon. *Literally*.

Wheeling Harlow down the hall toward the elevator, she waits till the doors close before the first tear falls. She always gets like this when we see Mack.

"Hey, it's all right, babe. He's got this," I say as I lean down and kiss her cheek. A part of her blames herself for what happened to him, but no one else does. None of this was her fault. It was that bastard, Titus. May he *not* rest in peace, but burn in hell.

"I know. It's just hard seeing him like that—bed ridden. I'm so used to seeing him up and about, lively and joyful."

"Give him some time. He'll be back to being a pain in my ass before you know it."

***

We've been in the truck for about fifteen minutes now and she hasn't even noticed that we aren't heading home yet.

I've been planning this since before she was taken, but it was supposed to be bigger and happier. But I think this is exactly what she needs right now. Something to mark her next step forward.

Pulling into the cemetery, she finally snaps outta whatever thoughts were keeping her prisoner inside her head and notices where we are.

"What are we doing here?" she asked, confused and a little leery.

"I wanted to show you something," is all I tell her, wanting it to be a total surprise.

Pulling in next to Toby and Blaze's bikes, she sees Dani and Sara standing by a plot.

Instead of asking more questions, she just waits for me to get the wheelchair out of the back and come around to her side.

She's still quiet as we make our way toward the others and I start to think that maybe this wasn't such a good idea. Maybe it's too soon. With everything she's dealing with and her PTSD, this probably isn't smart. But it's too late to turn back now.

When we stop in front of the two headstones, she gasps and starts to cry when she sees the headstones.

Hendrix Matthew McPherson–
Loving brother and protector

Rayanne Marie Gregerson–
Loving sister and friend

We all stay quiet for a while as she soaks this all in. She only mentioned doing something like this in passing, probably never thought I'd take what she told me and make it real this fast. If she only knew it was ready weeks ago.

Finally, she speaks. "When did you do this?" She hasn't lifted her eyes from the stones but I don't mind.

"While you were in the hospital," I say, and it's not a complete lie, I did set most of it up then.

"But why?" she asks, though I don't see how she doesn't already know.

Stepping around her and kneeling so I'm in front of her, I make sure she looks at me before I reply. "Because, babe. You deserve this. *They* deserve this. After you mentioned it to me, I wanted to do this for you. I thought it would be the perfect place for you to come to be close to them, to talk to them when you want to. And because I love you, Harlow."

Now she's crying even harder, but I think they are tears of joy, not tears of sadness. She'll always miss her brother, just like I miss my father, but she can finally heal. And I'll be there every step of the way.

"Thank you," she cries, then leans forward so she's in my arms.

"You're welcome, Harlow," I say, then pull back so she can look in my eyes as I say the next part. "I'll do anything to make you happy, to keep you safe, and to give you everything you ever want and deserve. I love you." Then I lean forward and kiss her on the lips.

Nobody says much, well, we don't really say anything at all. We bow our head and each stay silent but supportive. This is for Harlow. It's for her brother and their adoptive sister. They deserve so much more than a small gathering, but it's the best we could do with what we were given. I just hope it'll be enough for Harlow. I want this to be a place she can come to when she wants to be close to her brother.

When I feel her shoulder start to shake under my hand, I decide to say a few words for her. I don't know what they hell I should say, but I need to do this for my girl.

Clearing my throat, I start, "I didn't know either of you, but I know by what my woman has said that you were pretty amazing people. You had a shit hand dealt to you and for that I'm sorry. But I also want to thank you for protecting Harlow. What you both did saved her, and for that, I owe you my life."

Harlow silently continues to cry, but she's looking up at me like I'm her salvation. And fuck me, I want to be that for her. I want to be her every-fucking-thing. I don't know what I would do without her or what I would have done if something tragic had happened to her like what happened to her brother and foster sister. I meant what I spoke, I owe them my life for what they did for her. For protecting her when I wasn't able to.

Knowing what I need to do, I lift my eyes from Harlow's and stare at the headstones before me. "I owe you my life, but my life is connected to your sisters now. So I'll pay my respects a different way." Looking back to Harlow, I make sure she understands what I'm saying, why I'm doing it, and I pray she understands. "I swear to you, I will make that bastard pay for what he did to Hendrix and Rayanne. I will make him suffer. And I will make sure that he is unable to do to another child what happened to your brother and sister. I promise you, baby." I end my promise directed at Harlow.

At first, she doesn't say anything. She doesn't blink or give me any idea what she's thinking. But just when I start to panic, thinking I really fucked up this time, she grabs my hand and pulls me closer to her. "We'll make him pay together." Then she seals her promise with a kiss.

Pulling away, I look deep in her eyes and see that this is the closure she needs. It's not the funeral or service. It's not forgiving her brother. It's avenging him.

Nodding, I kiss her once more before standing silently behind her while she thanks everyone for coming. I would do anything for this woman. I would go to the end of the earth to make sure she has what she needs. I'd do anything to make her happy, even help her seek out revenge. I'd risk it all defying destiny, cause she's worth it.

I'd die for this woman, but I also live for this woman too. It's like my father always said, "You don't know what you live for until you know what you'll die for."

ACKNOWLEDGMENTS

I mostly want to thank my family. They dealt with me when I was tired and cranky from staying up all night writing. They talked me through some of these scenes and helped me make sense of what I was trying to put across. And they stood behind me and never lost their faith in me. Thank you all so much. I love you.

I also want to thank my fans. I know it's been a long road and you've all waited so patiently for this book. Thank you all for being so understanding when the release got pushed back because I signed with Limitless Publishing. It means the world to me that you all supported me and helped me achieve my dream of being a published author.

I also want to thank my cousin for helping me with some of the emotions that were in the book. I wanted it to feel as real as possible and having firsthand experience, you agreed to help me. Even though it was probably hard for you, thank you all your help. I hope I did you proud.

ABOUT THE AUTHOR

I grew up in a small town in Iowa. I have 2 older sisters and amazing parents. Growing up, I was always a daddy's girl, hanging out with him in the garage, fishing, and building stuff. I loved to play softball and swimming, but reading, telling stories, and writing were my passion, even at a young age. I took a break from writing for a while, but you could always find me with a book in my hand.

I have three children—two boys and a girl. They are my whole world. Even when I'm having the worst day ever, they brighten up my day and make me smile.

A few years ago, there was this story that would always play out in my head and no matter how many times I went through it, from beginning to end, it would never fade. So I decided to put it on paper. I didn't plan on publishing it, but when it was almost done, a friend asked to read it. She said it was a story that needed to be shared. And that's what started my writing career.

I love all genres of books, and even though I started with writing MC Romance, I have a whole book of ideas, so you can expect more from me than just MC, though romance is in my blood.

Even though I currently work two jobs, my ultimate dream is to become a full time author. I want to be able to spend my days filling pages with stories. I want to be the reason people find a reason to smile or laugh from lines on a page. Reading a book allows me to live in someone else's shoes, even if only for a few minutes. It's a way to leave my life and troubles behind and I want to be help others do that as well.

Don't forget…

If you haven't already, check out the first two books in the Forsaken Sinners MC Series.

PLUS, don't miss the Forsaken Sinners MC Novella!

Rewriting Destiny–Dani and Zane's story and prequel to the series.

Fighting Destiny–Toby and Sara's story.

Born into Destiny–Dani and Zane's story continued.

Coming soon…

Owning Destiny–Mack's story.

www.ingramcontent.com/pod-product-compliance
Lightning Source LLC
Chambersburg PA
CBHW030245200626
46816CB00002BA/511